D1024725

VENGEANCE
AT QUIET CREEK

VENGEANCE AT QUIET CREEK

•

Art Isberg

AVALON BOOKS
NEW YORK

PRINTED IN THE UNITED STATES OF AMERICA
ON ACID-FREE PAPER
BY HADDON CRAFTSMEN, BLOOMSBURG, PENNSYLVANIA

This book is dedicated to my wife, Ruth Dolores,
for her love, support and the many Quiet Creeks
we've camped on over the years.

Chapter One

Freedom's Breath

The echoing footsteps of Raffe Latimer flanked by two uniformed prison guards rang hollow against the gray stone walls until the men stopped at the steel-barred gate and one man stepped forward to open the big lock. Once through, they turned down another hallway, this one brighter with sun streaming through high windows off painted walls. Raffe squinted, his eyes sensitive to the sudden glare.

Finally, the guards pulled him to a stop in front of a door with a polished metal sign plate that read WARDEN. They knocked respectfully until they heard a muffled voice on the other side say, "Come in." Stepping through, Raffe saw John Betterman seated behind a

1

large wooden desk sifting through a sheaf of papers without looking up. He instructed the prisoner to sit down and kept reading.

After a long silence, the warden finally looked up over the rim of his thick glasses, then took them off, leaning back in his creaky chair to appraise the man about to be released, pursing his lips slightly as he studied the emotionless face.

"Well Latimer . . . it looks like you actually did all your time without either getting yourself killed by the rest of that scum back down there, or shot by one of my guards trying to escape. Quite frankly, I didn't think you'd ever make it this far. In fact, I'm almost disappointed you did. I figured we'd get the pleasure of burying you out back in the bone yard, but I just might get that chance yet. Men like you don't learn anything in here. They just get more hardheaded and mean. Then they step over the line again and I've got them right back here with me, but next time they stay for keeps. You see, it doesn't make me any never mind one way or the other. Sooner or later we'll meet again. I've seen dozens like you before, all losers who couldn't get their mind right no matter how much time they did. I saw that in you from the moment you came through the gate five years ago. I said to myself, well here's another hard-head who thinks he can do what he darn well pleases, but we'll just have to set him straight. You may think you can take the law into your own hands and be judge, jury, and hangman, but you can't because we aren't going to let you. Oh, you'll be back all right, and when you do I'll be waiting right here. I might even give you your old cell back just to make you feel comfortable, and if that don't work I'll stick you in solitary until you start seeing things and talking to yourself praying for just a sliver of sunlight to see what's going on around you, so the rats and cockroaches don't chew too much off of you each night when you try not to sleep. You want to make a bet I'll see you again right here and now?"

Betterman leaned forward, a cold forced smile tight across his lips, staring at the bearded man with the penetrating gray eyes across from him.

Raffe took in a slow breath, trying to control his emotions, hands still folded over his lap, as the guards on both sides of him smirked. Finally, he spoke.

"I came here five years ago with decent clothes, boots, thirty-five dollars, and a saddle and horse. That's what I want now that I'm leaving this stink hole you call a prison, and I want that release in front of you too."

The warden's face turned beet red as he rose from the chair and slammed a meaty fist down hard on the desktop, choking on the words stuck in his throat.

"You listen to me you . . . you murderer! You don't ever talk to me in that tone of voice—not inside this prison or out—you understand? I don't have to take that from any man and especially the kind of white trash you are. They should have put a rope around your neck for what you've done. Now get your sorry behind out of my office before I have you put right back where you came from, and fast!"

"I want that release in front of you. I'm entitled to it. It's the LAW you're so proud of upholding, remember?" Raffe demanded.

Betterman quickly scribbled his name across the document, then whisked it off the desk with the back of his hand onto the floor.

"You want it, pick it up along with the rest of the dirt, because that's what you're going to be worth once you get outside. Now get out of my sight!"

The guards escorted Raffe down the hall, then out into the open yard. They were still surrounded by high stone walls as they headed for the small guardhouse at the center of the tall, steel gate. At the guardhouse another man stepped out and handed Raffe a package, then keyed the final door leading to freedom.

"Where's the rest of my things?" Raffe asked, rummaging through the bag. "Where's my money, and what about my horse?"

"This is all you got coming. Warden's orders. Don't make any trouble over it or they'll haul you right back inside, hear?"

Latimer looked at the three for a moment, then turned and slung the bag over his shoulder, finally stepping outside into freedom as the gate clanged shut behind him. He started walking down the long, dusty, sagebrush-lined wheel track toward what he remembered was once the direction of a town.

Three hours later he heard the distant clatter of a stage and stopped, squinting back down the road. A rising dust plume was coming closer and closer, growing into a team of horses pulling a coach. The man on the seat up front handled a fistful of reins, then stepped off and held up his hand, signalling the stop. When the team finally danced to a halt, the driver looked down quizzically on the dust covered man.

"You out for a Sunday walk?" Burt Sugarman asked.

"Not hardly. I'm trying to get to the nearest town. What's its name, Leadville?"

"No, it's Leaderly, don'tcha know that?

What are you doin' way out here on foot, any-way—you lose your horse?"

"That and everything else I had. Listen, I don't have any cash on me, but I need a ride to town. Can I go up front in the box with you? It's that or I keep on walking."

Sugarman sized up the big man a moment longer, taking in the fact that he was unarmed, and finally nodded.

"All right, but when we get to town you'll have to pile off before I make the stage office. Old Johnson the manager don't go for giving out free rides, whether they're up here in the boot or back in the stage. Says he ain't running a charity line."

The coach lurched forward and the four-horse team quickly resumed their steady, ground-eating pace as the cool breath of wind played across Latimer's face, and he realized it was the first time he'd felt a cool wind like that in five, long years.

"So, what are you doin out here on foot?" Sugarman asked again as they rocked along. Raffe stared straight ahead until he finally made up his mind to answer.

"I just got out of the territorial prison back there." He glanced over at the driver. "I spent five years there. Does that bother you any?"

"No, no it don't. I don't hold prison against

any man that's done his time, but I'd sure like to think you weren't in there for murder or something like that after I stopped and picked you up, know what I mean? You might still have a little of that meanness left in you and want to take it out on the first person you see on the outside."

"If I did, I'd have to beat you to death with this clothes sack."

Both men looked at each other, then began laughing out loud, and Raffe suddenly realized that this was the first time he'd laughed in years.

When the stage wheeled into the outskirts of Leaderly, Sugarman reined it to a halt, talking to Latimer as he swung himself down.

"You know, Johnson might just be able to use a man at the station changing horses for the stage. The man he's got is aiming to quit pretty quick, and if you know anything about stock you might inquire about it. You'll need a job, won't you?"

"Yes, I will. At least long enough to put away some money before I move on, buy a horse and saddle, some other things. Where did you say he was at?"

Sugarman gave him directions, then tipped his hat, urging the coach forward. As it clattered away down Main street, Raffe stood and watched it go, then noticed the world around him he'd nearly forgotten. The street was lined on both sides by small houses. A few people were going about their business, and three young boys went running by. Suddenly, one of them pulled up short, staring at the stranger.

"Say mister, you got any change for some penny candy?"

"No son, I sure don't. I could use a little cash myself, but I can't help you."

The boy darted away to catch up to his pals, and as several passersby slowed to stare at him, Raffe realized that his threadbare clothes and unruly beard must make him look a little bedraggled. He quickly turned and walked away.

Wilford Johnson looked him up and down behind wire-rimmed glasses, then skeptically asked his first question.

"You really know anything about horses?"

"I do. I used to own a horse ranch of my own up north, and I handled a lot of stock for about ten years. I don't imagine taking care of stage animals is much different."

"And, if I decided to give you a try, do you have any place to stay?"

"No, I don't. I'll have to look around and

see if I can't work something out." Raffe answered.

"Work something out, huh?" Johnson pulled at his clean shaven chin, studying the tall man a moment longer.

"I'll tell you what. Jim Sornson, my man here, is quitting to head down south, and I could use someone to take his place. I've got a little shack out back, it isn't much but it might do, and if I give you a try you could stay there. It's right next to the corrals. I pay ten dollars a week, and you're on call any time I might need you day or night. I'll give you a try for a couple of weeks but if you don't work out that'll be it. You'll have to find something else. You want to give it a try?"

"You've got yourself a hand. Show me where I put my stuff."

Over the following days the stage manager quickly saw that his new man did indeed know horses as he'd said, and even knew a little doctoring for bruised or injured animals. He also grew to personally like the tall man who kept largely to himself and never said much about his past, except the fact that he'd once owned a ranch. As Johnson's respect grew, so did his curiosity, but Raffe was tight-lipped any time the subject came up.

Then one day three weeks later, Johnson approached him with an unexpected request while Raffe was feeding horses in the corral out back.

"Raffe, I need a big favor, and I need it pretty quick too. I'm going to run a night stage up to Elk City to pick up their gold shipment, and my regular guard Dan Hollister took sick and can't make the run. Would you consider riding guard in his place? I know you didn't hire on for it, but Burt's going to be doing the driving, and I can't have all that gold just left under the seat with him. If you'll do it, I'll furnish the weapons. You can handle a gun, can't you? I didn't see you come here with any."

Raffe put down the feed sack and looked at Johnson for a moment without answering.

"Isn't there anyone else in town who you can trust?" He asked.

"No, not really. I don't want the word to get around that we're going up there to the mine. That kind of gold makes people do foolish things, and I want to keep this quiet right here inside the business. I know I've kind of put you on the spot, but I don't have anyone else to ask."

Raffe thought about what happened the last time he'd had a fistful of six-gun, and the trial that sent him to prison for five long years, as he fought with himself for an answer.

"Listen, Wilford—I'm not the man you want for this. I'm not a deputy or lawman of any kind."

"You don't have to be. The company hires its own guards and we have every legal right to protect our own cargo, people, or anything else we carry. If I give you the job you don't have to worry about anything on that score. Now, what do you say?"

The tall man put both hands on his hips and took in a deep breath, looking back at the be-spectacled manager.

"All right, then. But let me see what you've got for weapons. I didn't come here with any-thing of my own."

"Good!" Johnson slapped him on the back as they turned and headed for the office. "I'll even give you a bonus for making the trip. Now, come on and I'll show you what I've got."

Later that evening Burt climbed up in the box with Raffe following right behind him, as Johnson gave last-minute orders.

"Remember what I said. Keep your eyes open on the way back once you've got the strongbox. I don't expect any trouble, but you never know. If you make good time you should be back by early morning, and tell Wells I said hello. I'll see you tomorrow."

Sugarman started the horses forward with a snap of the reins, and the empty coach disappeared down the nearly empty and shadowy main street. The long ride out of town under the blazing stars was cold and silent, and each man pulled his collar up high against the night and wrapped a heavy scarf around his neck and nose to try to keep out the chill. Later, Raffe leaned over to Sugarman.

"How far is it to Elk City?"

"Oh, about twenty miles. We should get there sometime around midnight, or maybe one in the morning. Say, you think you got enough shotgun there? That sawed-off double barrel across your lap sure ain't meant for birds, is it?"

"Johnson didn't have much else. Just this scatter gun and a rifle and pistol. I took this and the pistol, but it's been a long time since I've had my hands on weapons of any kind."

"I'll bet not with you being locked up like you were. Did you ever tell him about the time you spent in prison?"

"No, I didn't. I thought about it, but didn't. It would just make trouble for me at a time when I don't need any more."

"Well, you don't have to worry none about

me. I ain't going to say anything. What's done is done, and it's best to just leave it that way."

In the wee hours of morning, the stage finally pulled up in front of the office of Anaconda Mine. Clay Wells, the foreman, stepped out of the door followed by three other men.

"How was the ride up, Burt?" he asked as the driver stepped down to stretch and shake hands. Wells suddenly noticed that the usual gun guard wasn't on board.

"Where's Hollister?" He asked, and Burt explained, briefly introducing Raffe.

"Must be something going around. One of my men here, Dobie Grimms, is riding back with you to see Doc in town. Says he's been down sick with stomach cramps for three days and can't work. Maybe the old sawbones can give him something to clear him up."

"Johnson didn't say anything about taking on riders." Burt said. "Especially carrying gold like this."

"It's all right. He's one of my own men. He just came to work for me a couple of months ago, but he can make a pick ring like a bell, and I want him back here all in one piece and ready to work. We'll get the strongbox loaded up and you can get going, unless you want to come in for a cup of coffee before you pull out."

"No, we'll make tracks soon as we can. First I need to water the horses, then we'll pull out. I want to be back in town by early morning if I can, so go ahead and get your man out here."

The strongbox was loaded under the front seat, and the moaning passenger helped on board. After a brief watering Burt wheeled the big stage around and raised his hand in good-bye. Then the coach rattled off down the canyon, disappearing into the black of night.

For the first half-dozen miles down the long grade the going was easy, the team clipping along at a steady pace. But then the narrow, rutted road began winding uphill around sharp curves into an ever-steepening grade, and the team began pulling slower and slower, heading for the summit half an hour ahead. When the team finally approached the top they were down to a lunging pull, the animals blowing heavily as Sugarman sent his whip cracking among them to gain the top.

Just as they reached the peak, two riders spurred their horses out onto the road from the darkness and ordered the stage to stop, the soft glow of starlight glinting off their pistol barrels leveled at Burt and Raffe.

"Tie off them reins and throw that damn gold box down here!" one demanded. In the same instant their ailing passenger threw open the door and leaped to the ground, suddenly recovered, his six-gun extended in front of him.

"Stand up, both of you, and lift that strong-box out with both hands where we can see' em!" Grimms ordered.

"You're making a big mistake," Sugarman tried to say to the trio, but was instantly shouted down.

"Get it up here or I'll blow both of you off that seat!" One of the mounted men edged close now, and Raffe started to stand while his left hand reached down for the double-barrel stuffed between the seat and Sugarman. As he came full up he suddenly swung the sawed— off 12 across his hips, pulling off one barrel in a blinding flash of flame that nearly decapitated Grimms. He then instantly wheeled around and sent the second load into the nearest rider. Double—ought buckshot cut deep into the highwayman's chest, driving him completely backwards off his horse as both animals reared and danced to the sudden roar of explosion.

Burt ducked down under the seat as the last robber fired wildly at both men but missed on his twisting mount, while Raffe jerked the six-gun from under his coat firing once, twice, and a third time, until the last robber too hit the ground, rolling in pain and begging not to be shot again. Both men came down off the seat, quickly checking the two dead men, then walked over to the one still breathing.

"Don't shoot . . . I'm done . . . for," he gasped, blood already soaking through his heavy coat, as Raffe kept the long-barreled pistol trained on him. Then Raffe bent low to question him.

"Who put you up to this? Tell us while you still can, or you'll end up in hell."

"I'm goin' there any . . . way, so I guess it . . . don't make any difference . . . now. It was Grimms. He thought up the . . . whole thing, but now he got us . . . all killed. Tell my . . . brother . . . tell him. . . ."

There was a bloody gurgle, then the last man lay still under the cold, starry night as Sugarman slowly stood back up and looked at his partner.

"Jeez, Raffe, where'd you learn to handle guns like that?"

"It doesn't make any difference, Burt. We're both still breathing and aren't full of holes, that's all that matters."

"Well sure, but gosh a'mighty that was quick as lightning. How'd you know you could pull it off without getting us both killed?"

"I didn't. But I knew that I wasn't going to wait and see if these three were going to gun us down soon as they got their hands on gold either. Then, that would be us lying on the ground instead of them. It was just reflexes, that's all. I didn't have time to think about it."

"Reflexes? If that's what it was it was the kind only a lawman, or maybe a gunslinger, might have. You ain't never been a lawman before have you?"

"No, and I'm not a gun hand either, so don't waste anymore time worrying about it. Let's get these three loaded up in the baggage rack and tie off their horses. I'm sure your sheriff back in town will want to know all about what happened here, and you just tell him the straight of it, because I can't afford to be sent back to the state penitentiary again. Now let's get going."

It was well after sunup when the stage pulled back into town, and the three horses pulled behind the coach immediately got the attention of people already on the street who called to Sugarman asking about it. Wilford Johnson heard the commotion too and came outside to see his vehicle go right by the office. Burt yelled over to him.

"They tried to rob us! We're heading for the sheriff's office. Meet us over there."

By the time the stage came to a stop a crowd was already gathering, and when Lonn Thorn-

bourough stepped out of his office, the questions were flying fast and loud. Raffe and Burt
stepped down and took the sheriff around back,
where they unbuckled the baggage rack and
explained what happened.

"Would you look at that," someone re-
marked. "All three shot dead as a doornail!"

Thornbourough looked the bodies over, then
looked back to Raffe.

"You do all this?"

Raffe nodded, and the star man reached back
to turn over one of the dead men.

"That's one of the McCanlis boys—Jake's
son. They live out in the hills about ten miles
from town. He's going to be real unhappy with
you when he finds out you killed Orrin, here.
They're all a pretty wild bunch, but this is the
first time I ever heard of any of them trying to
rob a stage. As for these other two, I don't
know who they are. I guess you'd better come
into the office and tell me all about it, and
about yourself too. You're new around here,
aren't you mister?"

An hour later when Raffe left the office and
started back across the street to the stage depot,
people still on the street stopped to watch him
pass with awe and some fear. Already the word
had spread that this newcomer Raffe Latimer
was the man who'd shotgunned three men to

death in as many seconds. This was exactly the kind of thing he didn't want to happen here in Leaderly all over again, same as it had someplace else once before and sent him to Oklahoma Territorial Prison. That night, as he lay in bed listening to the wind whistling through the leaky shack, he'd already made up his mind what he had to do.

Chapter Two

Long Trail North

"Leaving, what do you mean, you're leaving? Now listen, I know those killings must be unsettling, but they were trying to rob us for gosh sake. You had every right to stop them. If you didn't they would have done the same thing to you. Can't you see that, Raffe? Don't let this get to you. Just settle down and let it pass for a while. It'll get better with time," Johnson tried counseling him.

"There's no living with a killing, at least not for very long, even when it's a holdup. It always causes the kind of trouble that keeps on coming back. The best thing for me is to gather up my gear and clear out, and that's what I mean to do."

"But you're just getting settled in here. You've got a good job, and I want you to stay on. Are you really ready to give all that up and just walk away that easy? For what—where would you go—do you even know yourself?"

"I'm going to head back up north to Colorado where I came from, or at least that's where I used to live . . . once. I knew a few people up there if they're still around."

"Would you please listen to me? Why don't you just give it a few more days, maybe a week or two, then see how you feel?" Johnson still tried to dissuade him.

"No. This will be my last week. I'll draw my pay Friday. That's the way it's going to be." Raffe started for the door, then stopped for a moment before going out.

"I could use a horse and saddle if you've got a mind to sell me one. If not, I'll go down to the livery."

"Yes, yes." Johnson shook his head, staring at the floor. "Pick out what you like. I guess that's the least I can do, but I still don't understand why you're doing all this, it just doesn't make any sense. But you're so darn bull-headed . . ."

"Thanks." Raffe said, pulling the door closed behind him.

That Friday he was tying saddlebags on his

horse when Burt Sugarman came out the back door of the stage office.

"Well, it looks like you're just about ready to go." He approached Raffe, smiling broadly at the big man.

"Yeah, pretty near. This is the last of it, but I didn't have much to start out with." Raffe turned toward his friend, extending his hand.

"Listen, Raffe. If you ever get back down this way again I expect you to look me up, hear? I mean, I ain't exactly thrilled by you pulling up stakes and leaving like this. I was just getting used to you. I mean, we made a pretty good team you and me, and now we're bustin' up too darn quick to suit me. Know what I mean?"

"I do, Burt, but this is for the best. I never planned to settle down here. I'm just leaving a little faster than I thought, that's all."

"I guess that holdup and the killings kinda changed things, didn't they?" Burt suddenly got serious.

"Yeah, it did, but it always does one way or the other, and it doesn't make any difference who's right or wrong either. If I stay around here, McCanlis or his brothers will only come looking for more trouble, and they'll be some trouble for sure."

"I know you ain't scared of them, not after

that night on the road. You saved my neck and your own too. If you hadn't been so handy with that scattergun, we coulda both been pushing up daisies by now, just like them other three."

"It ain't a matter of scared. I just don't want anymore gunplay around here. You remember where you picked me up on the road that first day? Remember where I'd just got out of after five years? If I stay here, that's where I'll end up being hauled back to, and I'm not going to let that happen, not for anything or anyone. I guess I better get going." He swung up into the saddle.

"Say, you still ain't carrying any weapons. I got an old hog leg out at the house used to belong to my brother. If you want it we could swing by and pick it up?"

"No, I'll likely buy something when I get further north. Take care of yourself now, Burt. Keep them horses in line."

Sugarman smiled and waved, watching him ride off until he turned the corner out of sight heading for main street, then he turned back for the office shaking his head. Strange man that Latimer, and one he hated to see leave so soon.

Raffe rode north for nearly a week before reaching the small town of Peytonville where he pulled up in front of the only dry goods store, then dusted himself off before going in for supplies. As he approached the counter his eyes fell on a brand new rifle that was resting on wooden pegs on the back wall. The proprietor was quick to see his interest and a chance for a sale.

"That's the new Winchester lever gun." He turned, lifted it, then turned back to Raffe. "No loading each round, just work the lever like this, and you're ready for another shot. It's a beautiful thing, isn't it? Makes you wonder what they'll think of next."

Raffe turned the rifle in his hands, then threw it to his shoulder, sighting down the long, steel blue barrel.

"I'll take it, and two boxes of shells, and let me see that .45 down there in the case too." He pointed.

The clerk quickly retrieved the pistol and handed it over the counter. Raffe cocked and recocked the hammer, releasing the trigger to get the feel of the action as it snapped down.

"This one too, and I'll need some dry goods, beans, coffee, and some hardtack if you have any."

"We certainly do, in fact my wife even makes it herself, and I've just got a fresh batch. Now you pick up what you like while I figure all this up." He began scribbling on a notepad, and when Raffe left the store he was loaded down with new weapons and enough food to keep him on the trail for at least another week if he didn't run into a town.

One evening three days later, Raffe had just built a small fire and dug the coffeepot and some food out of his saddlebags, when a distant voice suddenly floated in from out of the gloom.

"Hello, the camp. I'm coming in!"

He quickly moved to pick up the Winchester, then took several steps away from the fire, trying to adjust his eyes to the dark, when he heard hoofbeats coming closer. He made out a lone rider mounted atop a big roan.

"Now, don't get too touchy with that long gun, this is only a social visit. If it was anymore than that it would have already been over with you, standing around wide-open by that fire like that."

The stranger finally stepped down, and Raffe quickly appraised him and his outfit as he came closer to the light. That one look answered a lot of questions without Raffe needing to say a word. The man was average height and slender, wearing a flat-brimmed black hat, long leather overcoat, and striped pants tucked into

expensive, knee-high leather boots that still
had some of the shine of town left on them.
As he reached the fire he extended a gloved
hand, and Raffe saw a pair of pearl-handled
pistols snug in a silver-studded leather gun belt
as his coat opened slightly. He finally, got a
good look at the stranger's face, which sported
a thin, pencil-line mustache topped by a
straight nose and unblinking blue eyes.

"Name's Quick—Johnny Quick. I saw your
fire back there and decided to swing over. I
didn't expect to see anyone else out here. I
don't imagine you did either, by the way you
went for that rifle."

"No, not exactly," Raffe answered, still un-
sure whether to trust his sudden guest.

"Well, if you want to share some of that coffee and hardtack, I've got a little "red-eye" in
my saddlebags to wash it down with. You're
not just going to stand there and eat it all while
I watch, are you?" Raffe's smile grew a little
broader as Quick needled him good-naturedly.

"No, you go ahead and pull the cork. I
wouldn't want you to starve to death way out
here away from the last fancy restaurant you
probably ate in," Raffe joked back.

Slowly, over the next hour, the two men
sized each other up as they ate and drank, each
revealing as little as possible about himself ex-

cept for one thing: Both realized without discussing it that the other had been around guns and knew how to use them for far more than shooting rattlesnakes for target practice. Finally, Raffe asked Quick the question that had been on his mind since he rode in.

"You don't exactly look like you're used to working stock or horses dressed in that getup."

"Cattle? You kidding?" He laughed out loud, throwing his head back. "No, I don't do that kind of work. Too smelly and dirty. I leave that to others."

"I guess you don't—you're not exactly dressed for it." Raffe smiled. "What do you do then?"

"Let's just say I work for important people of means on assignment, and I travel a lot."

"It must pay pretty good." Latimer nodded at his fancy clothes.

"Well, yes, it does, but I offer a lot in return too. They get their moneys worth—every red cent—if you know what I mean."

"I believe I do. I probably knew it when you first rode in here. You hire out those fancy six-guns on your belt, right?"

Quick never took his eyes off Raffe, remaining silent for a moment longer as a slow, thin smile spread across his face.

"Why don't we just say I provide a 'service,'

and a valuable one at that, that certain people are willing to pay for. For example, let's say that a couple of dirtbags have been burning their brand over someone else's, and the local cattleman's association can't catch them. Then they call on me and I make them . . . disappear, and there's no more trouble. Or maybe some two-bit sheriff is as big a crook as the people he's supposed to be throwing in jail, and local city council can't get rid of him because they're buffaloed by him or others he has working for him. Then when I receive my retainer, I ride in there and have a little talk with the sheriff, and if that doesn't work I'll call him out in front of everybody and settle it right then and there. Townspeople aren't going to have me arrested for that because they're paying to get rid of him, so it's taken care of and everyone is happy with the results."

"So, you're a hired gun, plain and simple. Seems like a pretty touchy way to do business to me."

"You'd think so, but most men aren't going to draw on anyone when it comes right down to it, not unless they've used guns before. The man who isn't sure, who hesitates even for just a split second, he's dead where he stands. A lot of men talk big and shoot off their mouth, but when it comes down to putting their life on the line, they back off. Besides, don't tell me any of this bothers you, carrying around a brand new Winchester and that shiny six-gun. You don't need those to walk behind a plow horse, and you could use some advice on how to dress a little better. You almost look like a farmer the way you're covered up."

Raffe leaned back on the saddle he was using for a pillow and studied his cocksure companion, the flickering fire playing across both their faces.

"Well, I just sort of decided I wanted them. It's been a long time since I had my hands on any weapons, but I don't use them to make myself a living, not like you. Maybe you're not too far off on the farmer idea. I used to own a horse ranch up north a few years back, but then I lost it."

"See, I can read a man's character like a book. I told you you looked like a farmer." Quick laughed again. "Well, I tell you what. I'm going to get some shut-eye for an early start tomorrow. If you want, we could ride along together at least as far as we're going. Maybe I could teach you a few things, know what I mean?"

"Teach me, huh? I doubt that. You don't

look like you'd last two days out here on your own. It's too dirty and smelly for you, remember?"

In thirty minutes the dwindling fire had melted into a pool of glowing orange, and both men were sound asleep, wrapped in wool blankets against the chill night air.

Raffe woke early, tossed back his cover, and poured a canteen full of water to get the coffee going over the rekindled fire. When the aroma drifted over to Quick, he stirred a little, then slowly rolled over and squinted through sleepy eyes.

"Tell me when you've got the bacon and eggs ready . . . and be sure the toast isn't burnt black. . . . I don't like burnt toast, and no butter on it either," he chided the big man.

"Coffee is black and hot in about ten minutes. Get up or ride out of here empty," Raffe needled him right back, but there was something about his new camp mate that he liked, even though he had no intention whatsoever of telling him so.

Quick finally rolled over and sat up, rolling his blanket up, then pulling on his tall boots and running his fingers through his hair.

"What a man needs is a decent hotel with a good featherbed and restaurant, instead of rolling around on the ground like some cursed horned toad. You've been out in the brush too long, Latimer. In fact, the next town we come to I think I'll take you in and buy you a real meal, instead of drinking this oily coffee you call breakfast!"

"Will you? Well, what makes you think there's a town anywhere around here?"

"Cedar City is about another two-day's ride from here. When we get there I'm going to take a long hot bath, buy a box of good cigars, then have myself a good meal and an aperitif or two."

"A what?" Raffe cocked his head.

"An aperitif—a drink, good whiskey, you know what I'm talking about? You need an education in the finer things in life, you know that? What have you been doing—living in a cave?"

"No, but you're not too far off," Raffe answered. Quick turned his head and waited for the rest of the answer, but it never came. Raffe remained silent, then drained his cup and kicked the fire out.

"Let's get going."

When they rode into Cedar City, Quick headed for the only hotel in town and got a room, tossing a pair of twenty-dollar gold pieces across the counter at the manager.

"Have a boy fill two tubs with hot water and

plenty of soap, and bring me a bottle of your best whiskey, none of that rotgut they serve at the bar."

"Yes sir," the bald man answered, scooping up the coins. "I'll have it ready for you by the time you unload your gear and find your room upstairs. Will there be anything else I can get you . . . ah . . . gentlemen?"

"Not right now." Quick turned back toward the front door.

Later, as both men sat soaking in tubs with suds up to their chests, Quick lit a cigar, then sipped at the whiskey glass.

"See, Latimer, this is how life is supposed to be lived, not out rolling around on the ground at night. You starting to get the hang of it yet?"

"Yeah, it's O.K." Raffe turned to retrieve his glass, and Quick caught a glimpse of deep scars crisscrossing his back. Quick wondered if he'd get an answer even if he asked, then gave in to the temptation.

"Say, what's all that on your back—someone take a whip to you?"

Raffe settled back down in the tub, glancing at the man next to him without answering for a moment. Then he decided he just might owe him one after Quick paid for room, board, and this steaming hot bath.

"I got them back down south in territorial prison. They're a little gift from the warden anytime you get out of line and break the rules. If solitary doesn't work then they go to rawhide. They call it, "getting your mind right"— at least that's what Betterman, the warden, liked to call it. I used to dream about handcuffing him to a set of bars and whipping him to pieces, just so I could ask him if his mind was right yet, but that was just a dream."

"Looks like you must have spent a lot of time going against the grain. I figured you were kind of hardheaded about the first fifteen minutes after I met you, and I guess I figured right again, huh? What were you in for?"

Raffe let out a long breath, knowing he shouldn't have answered the questions in the first place. Then he took another drink and set the glass on the edge of the tub.

"It isn't worth talking about. It's over and done with. I've got other things on my mind now."

"C'mon, don't back out now. What were you in for? It sure as hell wasn't for stealing penny candy, was it?"

He ran the hot washcloth across his chest, wishing he'd just kept his mouth shut as Quick pressed him again.

"I killed a man in a gunfight. It was a fair

fight, I called him out, but the sheriff and two of his deputies said I bushwhacked him and the judge believed them. I got five years because his gun had two spent shells in it, or they probably would have swung me from a rope. I could never figure out why that sheriff lied like he did. Maybe one of these days I'll find out?"

"So, you called him out, huh?" Quick's face lit up with a smile. "And here you been calling me a hired gun!" He laughed, satisfied with himself.

"It wasn't for hire. It had to do with my family, nothing fancy like you. Now let's just drop the whole subject and get out of these tubs before I get waterlogged."

After dinner in the hotel restaurant the two men sat a bit longer having a smoke while Quick eyed the crowded poker room through a curtained partition.

"You know, if you're going to ride with me you ought to go out and buy yourself some decent clothes so you look a little respectable when we're out on the town like this," Quick needled him again.

"Well, first of all, I'm not riding with you, remember? I said I was heading north and you threw in with me. I didn't ask you to. And second, I'm not trying to impress anyone with what I wear. Besides, if I had to buy everything

you've got on I'd probably be broke by tomorrow morning."

Quick loved these little exchanges and
laughed at his new-found friend's fast come-
back.

"That's what I like about you, Latimer, you
keep everything so damn simple, just like yourself. Now, I don't suppose you know how to
play poker, do you, because there's a nice fat
game going on in the next room, or do I have
to teach you that too?"

"Nope, you play. I'm not interested. I'm going to finish this drink, then head upstairs and
get some shut-eye. You play with that bunch,
they'll clean you out. Half of them are probably playing for house anyway, just waiting for
someone like you to come strolling in."

"Oh, there's not much of a chance anyone
is going to clean me out." Quick got to his feet,
straightening his vest. "I'll see you later . . .
'preacher.' Yeah, that's a good name for you
because you sound just like a Sunday school
preacher I had when I was a kid, always telling
me what I shouldn't do. My mother used to
make me go every Sunday until she found out
I was skipping out and heading for town instead. Mama had good intentions, bless her, but
they just didn't work for me. You probably had
good intentions too, until you took that man

down and got sent to prison, huh?"

Raffe didn't respond, he only looked up with that deadpan stare of his as Quick slapped him on the back and then walked toward the poker room.

"Gentlemen," he said, pushing the curtains aside and stepping in. "I believe they call this game poker, don't they? I see you have an empty seat—mind if I sit in?"

Near midnight the lobby and restaurant were silent and dark and the game had dwindled to just three players, although many more men stood around the table to watch the action. The dealer and Quick had most of the money, and the third man, a local businessman named Horace Johns hung on, trying to ride out a long losing streak that nearly had him broke.

The dealer, Benny Fane, shuffled the cards in quick succession, then flipped them expertly around the table, calling five-card draw again. Johns took a quick look at his cards and realized that he had the best hand he'd been dealt in over an hour, so he opened with twenty dollars. Quick saw the bet and raised another twenty and Fane matched the pot, calling for cards. Both he and Quick drew three, while Johns stood pat. Now Johns bet another twenty and the dealer saw the bet, raising thirty-five more to try to drive Johns out. Quick matched both bets and upped the ante another twenty. One of Johns' friends who was standing behind him leaned down and whispered in his ear.

"Get out, Horace, neither of them is going to back off."

Johns ran his hand across his forehead, still studying his cards, then looked across the table at both men.

"Everything I've got is in the pot. I'd like to stay in for what's here, but I can't see another raise."

Fane glanced at Quick, sure his strategy had worked, but Quick only shrugged and said, "That's okay with me, let him stay. It's your bet." He nodded back at the dealer.

Fane pushed out fifty this time, and Quick matched right back.

"I call. Everyone turn them over," he said, sipping at his whiskey.

"I've got two pair!" Johns glanced quickly at the men, praying it would be enough.

"Full house, Horace. Eights over deuces." Fare spread his cards out, looking across as Quick pushed his over.

"Not enough, boys, I've got four little sixes."

Johns slumped in his chair, flat broke, then took a deep breath. "I've had enough for one night. I'm going home." He slowly got to his feet, looking down at Quick. "Mister, you're the luckiest son of a gun I've seen lately."

Then he walked out of the room. Fane watched him go, pulling at his chin in thought, still upset at losing once again to the fancily dressed newcomer.

"You still feel lucky?" He raised an eyebrow and looked at Quick.

"Yeah, I do. What do you have in mind?"

"What I've got here in front of me against your pile. They're pretty near the same, and I won't even ask for a count."

"Good enough, but let's just make it one hand. I want to get to bed before sunup if possible. I've got a touchy partner and he likes to get his sleep. What's your pleasure?"

"Five-card stud, nothing wild—straight poker, for all the marbles."

"Roll 'em out." Quick nodded, as Benny reached for a new deck.

"No. We play with the same cards. I don't want another deck. These have been good to me all night long, and I'm not going to turn my back on them now."

"They're beat up and bent. A man might be able to "read 'em" the way they are," Fane protested.

"You chose the game and the stakes. But I want the cards. Deal those or I cash in."

The dealer's jaw tightened as he tried holding his temper, then he shuffled the deck quickly and flipped them out, picking up his five and fanning them slightly, the big pair of aces jumping out at him as he looked across the table and smiled ever so slightly. Then he pushed all his cash to the center, locking eyes with Quick.

"Well, what have you got?" He rolled his up on the velvet tabletop. "I've got a pair of bullets straight up!"

"I believe three little five's beats your bullets, don't it? My pot." Quick scooped the money in, as Fane's face turned beet red and his pent-up anger finally boiled over.

"You know, Johns said you were the luckiest son of a gun he ever saw, but you've been pulling up those winners all night long and I'm not so sure it's just all luck!"

Quick looked across the table, still stacking his money with one hand while his other slowly slid down toward the .45 tucked in his gun belt.

"Let it go while you still can, Fane. If you can't stand getting beat then you ought to find another line of work, because if you make one more remark like that you'd better be prepared to stand up with something in your hand to back it. I'm not one of these local yokels that comes in here to play when they close up the store, or some cowhand in off a ranch who never played poker before except in a bunkhouse. Now shut up and take it like a man, if you've got that in you."

The dealer stood glancing red-faced at the onlookers around the table without saying another word, then turned to leave the room, but just as he reached the curtained partition he spun around with a derringer in his hand and someone yelled, "Look out!" Quick lunged sideways in his chair, throwing the card table up as he went down, rolling across the floor and pulling his pistol, both men firing simultaneously. Fane was blown completely back through the curtains and out into the dining room hall, two bullets in his chest.

When the gun smoke cleared Quick slowly got to his feet, looking down at the neat, .25-caliber hole in the shirt of his left arm, the blood already spreading into a bright red circle. Then suddenly everyone was yelling at once and someone said to go get the sheriff. Quick walked out into the hall and looked down at Fane, eyes still wide open in death.

Later, he sat at the righted poker table, a bar towel wrapped tightly around his arm, as Sheriff Todd questioned him about the whole affair and bystanders tried to get in on the conversation. Finally, the sheriff had had enough.

"Will the rest of you keep quiet, so I can get this story straight? Now, shut up!"

He turned back to Quick just as Raffe pushed his way through the throng of men. Quick's attention was diverted to Raffe with a knowing smile. The sheriff caught this, and twisted in his chair to size up the big man.

"You know this man?" He pulled a thumb toward Quick.

"Never saw him before," Raffe deadpanned, and suddenly Quick couldn't help but laugh out loud, startling everyone there and perplexing Todd even more.

The next morning, after he'd been tended to by a doctor, Raffe told his hard-gambling partner that he was moving on, and asked him if he could ride with his arm bandaged.

"Why sure I could, but I'm not leaving a winning streak like this, you crazy?"

"A winning streak? You've already caught a bullet and got half the town in an uproar over killing that dealer, and you're going to stay and keep playing?"

"Absolutely. You don't know much about cards do you? When they're falling your way you don't just walk away from luck like this. Besides, I've got plenty of time before I need to get to my next "job," and I like it here. Good food, soft beds, plenty of money floating around. You ought to stick around too preacher. You might even learn how to enjoy yourself."

"Not me. I'm saddling up this morning. I guess maybe we'll run into each other sometime if you don't get your head blown off by some sore loser."

"Have it your own way then, but where did you say you were headed?"

"Up north to a place called Quiet Creek. I used to live there once before I got sent south."

"Oh yeah, I remember now. Well, it's been fun, it just didn't last long enough. Too bad, preacher, I could have taught you how to roll those cardboards out and make some real money without even working up a sweat, but you want to go wallow in the mud." He shook his head.

"Not hardly. I just want to get back up to my own country. There's some things up there that aren't settled yet. Maybe this time they will be."

Quick stuck out his hand, gripping Raffe's and grinning with that thin, cold smile of his.

"Okay, preacher. I hope you find what you're looking for. But don't look too hard— you don't want to end up back in Oklahoma as a guest of the territory again, do you?"

"That isn't going to happen. I'll see you, Johnny."

Chapter Three

The Return

Far to the north in the mountain town of Placer City, a heated conversation was going on in the office of Sheriff Bart Hollister, his deputy Clint Richie, and Cyrus Slaughter, an old cattle rancher with a big spread that ran all the way up the valley to the lower end of Quiet Creek, and someone known for unbending, single-minded viciousness.

"The wire Clint picked up down in Kellsyville says they released Latimer from territorial prison about three weeks ago. We don't have to be too smart to figure out which way he's headed by now, do we?"

"I'm not so sure, Bart. After five years in the big stony and considering what happened to him and his brothers up here, he just might decide it's healthier to head off someplace else. There's nothing for him here but more trouble and he knows it." Richie stopped for a moment, rolled a smoke, then lit it. "Besides, what have we got to worry about anyway? He's just one man now."

"I'll tell you this," Cyrus cut in. "If he shows his face around here, I'll have my men run 'im off at the end of a whip! We got rid of him and his bunch once before, and I'm not going to put up with him again if he tries to come nosing around, not after we've got things set up just the way we want. If that darn judge in Kellsyville had done his job like he was supposed to, he'd have hung him instead of letting him sit in prison all this time thinking about everything. When I came into this country forty years ago we didn't have no judge, no juries, and no pettyfoggin' lawyers to muddy things up. A man was his own law, and what he could back up with a six-gun was his, period! Those that didn't have the stomach for it moved on to someplace else and I said good riddance. That's the way all this country was back then, and that's the way it should be now too. I didn't build up my spread by asking anyone if it was all right to take what country I could hold. I ran them darn Indians off and shot them that wouldn't leave. Now, I'm not going to put all that in jeopardy just because of one man. If you'da done it right, Hollister, none of this would have happened in the first place!"

"Listen to me, both of you. Let's just keep our shirts on and our mouths shut. We're in the clear about this whole deal, and that's the way we need to stay. If or when Latimer shows up, he's an ex-con, and the first time he spits on the wrong side of the street, I'll run him in. With a little luck I might even get him sent back down south, and this time he won't come out. We've got everything on our side, so let's not go and get all worked up about what 'might' happen. All right?"

"I still like my way better," Slaughter insisted. "Put the run on him the minute he gets within ten miles of here and keep him goin', and I've got the men to do it too. I even hired me a new man recommended by friends to deal with those damn squatters trying to stick a plow into my winter range up at the north end of Big Meadow. If it wasn't for you, I'da had them out of there by now my way." He leveled a finger at Hollister. "There's always a few that think they can just sit tight and eventually I'll let 'em stay on just like Latimer did, but that will be over pretty quick when my man arrives here. From what I'm told he's the best in the business at "persuading" people to move on or get planted, and I'm paying good money to see that he does."

"You just be sure he doesn't put me in a bad position with local folks here," the sheriff interjected. "I can't have someone riding around gunning people down just to get them off your place. That kind of trouble could bring in a U.S. Marshal from outside, and that's something we don't need."

"He's too good for that. He'll just have a little 'talk' with them and if they don't pull up and leave, then he gets serious. Don't you worry none. He knows how to make it look all legal-like."

"Clint, it's about time you made the rounds then went home for the night." Hollister pointed at the door.

"Yeah, Bart." Richie pushed out of the chair. "I'll see you two later, okay?"

After he closed the door, Slaughter leaned over close to the sheriff with narrowing eyes.

"You sure he's going to be all right if things heat up?"

"Clint does what I tell him to, and as long as he follows my orders there's nothing to worry about. He'll keep his mouth shut because he's in this as deep as we are."

"Well, he'd better, because I'm not going to have some ten-dollar-a-week tin star fold up on us if the going gets a little rough. He might be all right as long as he's got you to lean on, but I don't know about it when he's out on his own, especially if he ran into someone like Latimer."

"He's not going to have to. Now stop worrying about everything, will you?"

Over the next two weeks Hollister and his deputy walked the muddy streets of Placer City studying the face of each new rider who came into town without recognizing any of them. At night they went from bar to bar studying noisy patrons through dirty glass windows, yet never found the one man they were looking for and feared most.

Finally, one evening back at the office, Richie hung up his gun belt and turned to Hollister. "See, Bart. I told you he wasn't coming back here. He's had plenty of time to get here by now if he meant to."

"Maybe, maybe not. We'll just keep our eyes open. If he does show I want to be the first one to stop him and have a little 'talk.' You head on home now, and tell Betty I said thanks for the cookies."

But just as the deputy stepped out the door that evening, ten miles north of town a lone rider came out of dark timber. He reigned to a stop and looked down the long grassy slope toward a small cluster of buildings set against a big meadow. No light came from the ranch house windows, no telltale wisp of blue smoke curled up from the stone chimney. For several moments more the rider sat motionless, taking in the scene below as memories came racing back, faces and voices flashing through his mind until they seemed almost real. He knew this ranch, every log-laid wall, every deep-seated post and rail. He slowly edged his horse forward, his heart beating faster in his chest, as the first sliver of full moon pulled itself up over the jagged mountains to the east and illuminated the scene even further.

At the hitching post he slid down, wrapping the reins, then stepped up onto a creaky porch aged by neglect. He pushed the front door open and slowly stepped in as moonlight began flooding the darkened interior. Something tiny scurried away across the floor as he advanced across the log-beamed living room to a big stone fireplace on the far wall. Once, he remembered, it had blazed with snapping flames and warmth only a man who had built it with his own two hands could really appreciate, but now it stood cold and empty.

In the dining room, several chairs lay scat-

tered across the floor, and in the kitchen, the
old, cast-iron woodstove still sat in one corner,
though it was now home to a band of wood
rats. As a growing shaft of moonlight slid si-
lently across one wall, he pushed the back door
open and stepped out onto the porch. The barn
and corrals shone brighter now, and he was
even able to see all the way out across the
meadow to the dark mountainside that shel-
tered Quiet Creek. He stood stock-still and listened. Yes, there it was, the distant gurgle and
rush of the dancing stream as it wound its way
down the canyon into the black of night: the
sounds, sights, and smells he'd dreamed of as
he lay in a hard, prison bed for five long years.
Raffe Latimer had come home at last, but to a
home that was no longer his. Back inside he
sat on the cold stone fireplace hearth thinking
to himself. He'd made it all the way back
home, to ground he'd carved out with his own
two hands and that of his brothers too. Now if
he could just figure out some way to get it all
back.

That night he slept in the abandoned ranch
house, then woke at dawn and built a small fire
in the fireplace, heating a pot of coffee. He
then cleaned up and retrieved his saddlebags,
pulling out the new shirt and pants he'd bought
back in Cedar City. If Quick could only see

him now he'd bust a gut! Just like the dapper
man with the fast hands had said: "Clothes
make the man," and he'd need them this morning for what he had in mind. But first, he had
one stop to make.

The morning sun was high over the trees by
the time he pulled up outside a weed-choked
cemetery. He got down and began walking the
unkempt rows, reading names on markers until
he stopped and knelt down at a pair on the far
end near a sagging picket fence.

DEAN LATIMER	VIRGIL LATIMER
1834–1856	1829–1856
May he find peace now	His brother keeps him now

For a long time Raffe did not move. His mind
swirled remembering the ambush gunfight that
killed his brothers on the streets of Placer City,
and nearly took his life too. He remembered
every second of it like it was yesterday: the
way the three of them had ridden into town
after working on the ranch all day to go to the
dry goods store. They had pulled up and
stepped down, and had just been starting up the
stairs when four men had suddenly come up
behind them, guns drawn, claiming they had
"papers" for charges they knew nothing about
in another town miles away, and ordering them
to throw down their guns.

The brothers had protested, telling the bounty hunters they had the wrong men and to lower their weapons to no avail, until one of the whiskered four stepped up and reached for Dean's holster. In a flash, all hell broke loose as they wrestled for the weapon and it went off, sending Dean crumpling to the ground. Raffe and Virgil instantly drew their six-guns, firing a string of shots. Virgil took two bullets and fell to his knees, still shooting, as two of the bounty hunters went down rolling in the streets. Raffe continued to pump shots into them, but suddenly he felt a crashing blow to the back of his head. As he fell onto his back, the last thing he remembered seeing was Bart Hollister standing over him with a rifle in his hands—the rifle he'd clubbed him with.

The next thing he knew he was lying in a cell, handcuffed to a cot, with the sheriff and Clint Richie looking down at him. A warm trickle of blood ran down the side of his face as he tried to talk through a fog of semiconsciousness, with Hollister nearly shouting that he'd killed two men and would be tried for murder.

"They . . . weren't . . . law . . . men." He finally got out, trying to reach up and wipe the blood out of one eye, but unable to because of the cuffs.

"They were bounty hunters with legal papers, and you and your damn brothers shot them down!" Hollister was nearly beside himself with rage. "You been acting high and mighty ever since you rode in here a year ago claiming to homestead that ground up on Quiet Creek, when you knew all along that Cyrus Slaughter ran his stock on it for years. Now you've gone and went over the line, and I'm going to see to it that you don't get a second chance to make any more trouble around here or anyplace else. Your brothers are going to be buried out in Boot Hill where they belong, and it's just too darn bad you didn't end up there with 'em too! Clint, keep an eye on him while I head over to Doc's and see if that third man made it or not. If he moves so much as an inch, lay your gun barrel across his hard head again. Maybe we can save a judge and jury a big waste of time and public money. I'll be back pretty quick."

Raffe blinked back to reality, rubbing his forehead, then stood up and looked down at the weed-lined graves. All of his questions came rolling back: Who were those men who called themselves bounty hunters, and who set them on Raffe and his brothers? And what of Hollister? Why was he so quick to take sides against him? He hardly knew the lawman, and had said even less to him over the year he'd worked building his ranch on Quiet Creek. Why had Hollister been so anxious to get rid of him, even hoping he could get him hung? For five long years Raffe had asked these questions over and over again, but still none of it made any sense.

Finally, he mounted up and headed for town. As he rode out of the forest, still short of the main road, he saw the distant image of a buggy streak by with a runaway horse running hard. The carriage bounced and whipped dangerously from side to side, its single occupant obviously unable to control the animal. Raffe spurred his horse forward in hot pursuit.

As the big animal hit level ground on the main road, it began eating up the distance, drawing closer and closer to the buggy with each thundering stride until Raffe drew close enough to see a red-haired woman clinging to the reins, trying to haul the buggy to a stop. He kicked his horse up alongside the carriage, then rode up beside the wild-eyed beast, so close that he could lean down and take the reins in hand, laying into them as he pulled his own horse back, and eventually slowing down until they all came to a stop.

"You all right?" he asked, getting down but

still holding the buggy reins in one hand to keep the jittery horse from running again.

"Yes, I'm okay. For a while there I thought he was going to run all the way into town before he stopped. I don't know where you came from, but I'm certainly glad that you arrived."

The young woman stepped down from the carriage and walked up to him as he handed her the leathers.

"Better keep a good grip on him. It'll take him a few minutes before he calms down."

"I don't believe I know you," she replied, sticking out a gloved hand to shake his. "I thought I knew just about everybody around these parts by now."

"My name's Latimer, ma'am. Raffe Latimer. I . . . used to have a place up on Quiet Creek, but I haven't been around for a while."

"Latimer?" She stared at him with deep blue eyes, the hint of a smile on her lips. "I think I've heard my uncle mention that name."

"Well, who's your uncle?" he asked.

"Cyrus Slaughter. I finished school back east, and my mother sent me out here to 'see the west.' She laughed quickly at her own wild buggy ride. "My uncle owns a cattle ranch east of here. I've been staying there the last six months, but I don't think we've met, have we? Listen, I don't want to seem ungrateful, but

I've got an appointment in town and I don't want to be late. Thanks again for your help. I could have ended up in a ditch."

"I'll just ride along with you a ways to be sure that nervous horse of yours doesn't take off again. I'm heading that way too."

"Oh, I'm sorry. My names Jennifer Mitchell. My friends call me Jenny."

"Well, if you don't mind a little friendly advice, I wouldn't tell your uncle about all this."

"Why not? I told him I wanted to ride my own horse to town, but he said it wouldn't be ladylike." She laughed again, and Raffe liked the sound of it.

"Let's just say your uncle and I have our differences."

"I'm really sorry to hear that, Mr. Latimer, because you saved me from what could have been a terrible situation, and I know Uncle Cyrus would like to thank you for it, just like I have."

"I don't believe he would, ma'am. Believe me, it's best just left unsaid. You ready to try it again?"

When Placer City came into sight, Raffe tipped his hat and smiled quickly, then urged his horse ahead. Jennifer Mitchell watched him ride away. *What a strange man*, she thought.

There was something about him, something out of place, if that was the right word for it. Even when he'd talked to her it had seemed his mind was really someplace else. And why didn't he and her uncle get along? What was that all about? In her own way, she meant to find out.

When Raffe rode down Main Street, people on the boardwalk stopped and stared, but he kept his eyes straight ahead. Clint Richie had just gone over to the woodstove by the window to pour another cup of coffee from the pot on top when he glanced out the window and saw Latimer ride by. Instantly, he forgot about coffee and turned, calling out for Hollister upstairs at one of the cells, then vaulting up the steps.

As Raffe neared the bank on the corner, an old bearded man stepped out into the street.

"Raffe, it's good to see you back!"

"You're about the only one around here who seems to feel that way, but it's good to see you too, Dusty. It's been a long time."

"Too long!" Dusty called after him as he continued on.

At the bank he got down and tied off his horse, then looked up and down the sidewalk at people frozen in their tracks watching him. He went inside. Horace Eaverhardt, the bank president, was sitting at his desk studying a sheaf of papers when he heard the door open and close. He looked up to see Latimer coming around the counter toward him without waiting to be ushered in. For a moment the name stuck in his throat, even though he knew it as well as his own. He started to push the chair back and get to his feet, but Raffe stopped him, and he sat back down.

"Why, Mr. Latimer . . . I mean, Raffe, it's quite a surprise to see you back. . . . I mean, I didn't know you were . . . in this part of the country again. Sit down, make yourself comfortable. Can I have someone get you a cup of coffee? What . . . brings you here?" Eaverhardt pulled at his tie nervously.

"No, I don't want anything except some information. I want to know what happened to my place up on Quiet Creek."

"What do you mean, what 'happened' to it?"

"I want to know who bought out my deed after I was sent down south. Who owns it, Horace, and don't give me the runaround."

"Why Raffe, that information you should get down at the county office in Kellsyville, not here from me. It's a matter of public record, if you'll just ride down there and look it up. The bank has certain procedures we have to respect. I can't just . . ."

Raffe's hand slid across the desk, locking on the little man's jacket and pulling him hard against the oak desk.

"I said, who bought my place, and I'm not going to ask you again. I paid you and this bank nearly two thousand dollars toward my mortgage before my brothers and I had that shoot-out, and I want an answer now. I'm not riding to Kellsyville or anyplace else to get it. Spit it out, Horace."

"Ahhh, well, I believe that Mr. Cyrus Slaughter bought up the deed and paid off the balance, but it was done fair and square, according to law, Raffe. If someone can't pay off a place then the bank puts it up for auction, and that's what we did. Now, you may not like it, but that's the way . . ."

Raffe let go and got to his feet, looking down at the bespectacled man.

"That's all I wanted to know, Horace. I'm real glad you did it lawful-like. Do you have any trouble sleeping at night?"

"What?" the president asked, but Raffe didn't wait for an answer, and headed for the door.

Outside, he went down the steps and untied his horse. Suddenly, a voice shouted from the middle of the street behind him.

"Latimer!"

He turned to see Sheriff Hollister and Richie both leveling shotguns at him from forty feet away as bystanders scrambled for the cover of doorways.

"You just stand real easy now, and take that hog leg out of your holster, and throw it over here."

He paused, studying both men, as his hands went to his side.

"I've done my time, Hollister. You can't touch me now, and you'd better lower those scatterguns, because if you pull them off there's fifty witnesses right here watching you. You can't lie your way around a jury like you did before."

Hollister glanced quickly at the spectators peering from cover, then turned back to Latimer.

"I said get rid of that gun and stay away from the Winchester on your horse too!"

The two advanced, covering Raffe every step of the way, until the sheriff finally pressed the shotgun hard against Raffe's stomach and ordered Richie to lift his six-gun.

"Now, you're coming with me, by law. Get going, and if you take one step in the wrong direction I'll fill your back full of buckshot!"

The three marched down the center of the street until they reached the sheriff's office.

Once inside, Hollister muscled Latimer down the hall to the nearest cell, slamming the door shut and locking it behind him.

"This is where you belong. It's what you're used to, isn't it? The next time I give you an order you'd better obey it, mister, and right quick, or I'll have you on a prison wagon back to Oklahoma faster than you can say 'it'."

"What am I being charged with?" Raffe locked his hands around the cold steel bars.

"Disturbing the peace, returning to the scene of the crime, you name anything you want, because I can think up half a dozen more if I have to, and I'll make 'em all stick too. You had your chance to clear out, but you had to come back, didn't you, and try and stir up more trouble? You didn't have enough brains to just move on someplace else, and now you can just sit here until I'm good and ready to turn you loose, whenever that is!"

Hollister heard the front door open and Richie greeting someone in the outer corridor. He turned and started for the hall. Upon entering, he was surprised to see Jennifer Mitchell waiting for him, as the deputy stood off to one side and shrugged his shoulders.

"Why Miss Mitchell, what are you doing here? You've sort of come at a bad time. . . ."

"I saw what happened out on the street.

What are you charging Mr. Latimer with?"

"Mr. Latimer? Don't tell me you know this troublemaker? Why are you asking in the first place?"

"Yes, I know him, somewhat, and whatever you're charging him with I want to bail him out. Now, what did you bring him in here for?"

Both men stood and stared at the woman in amazement, then at each other, before Hollister finally answered.

"All right . . . I'm charging him with disturbing the peace, you satisfied now?"

"I am. And what's the bail for that?" she quickly shot back.

"Bail is . . . twenty-five dollars, but just wait a minute. Before you go any further with this. . . ."

Jennifer dug in her purse, then laid the money on the desk. "I want him out, now!" Her face flushed red with seething anger.

"Now listen to me for just a minute. Why in the world are you posting bail for him, anyway? He's a convicted murderer, did you know that? He's just got out of territorial prison. And what do you think your uncle is going to say when he finds out about this, huh? You don't know what you're getting yourself into, and you'd better think twice before you go any further."

"I said get him out here! I saw what you did out there on the street, and so did everyone else. In a real court of law you wouldn't last five minutes on a trumped-up charge like this. Now I've paid the fine, and don't worry about my uncle either. I want Mr. Latimer out of here."

"You're going to be sorry about this, you mark my words young lady!" The sheriff tossed Richie the keys, nodding back towards the cell block. A moment later, Raffe came out, looking first at the woman and then at Hollister. He'd heard the entire conversation.

"Get out of here, both of you, and you watch your step, Latimer." The sheriff pointed a finger at the big man. "I'll be watching you every minute you're in town here. You set just one foot down in the wrong place and I'll be right there to haul you in. Get the picture?"

"Give me my gun." Raffe pointed to the .45 still stuck in Richie's belt, as the sheriff withdrew it and then emptied all the cartridges out on the table, tossing it to him.

"There, you've got it, now get out of here, and remember what I said. There isn't going to be any second time for you. You're not wanted around here, if you haven't figured that out by now. If I were you, I'd saddle up and keep right on going."

Raffe took several steps toward Hollister, looking him straight in the eye, then holstered the empty pistol.

"You ever put a gun on me again, you'd better be ready to use it, because I will." His voice was low, almost a whisper. Then he and Jennifer turned and went out the door, walking back down the street toward Raffe's horse.

"You just put yourself in a bad way, you know that, don't you?" Raffe he asked, turning toward Jennifer.

"Maybe, but I'm not as worried about it as you seem to be. Did you really murder someone like he said?"

"Not the way he made it sound. There was a whole lot more to it than that."

"I'd like to hear about it, if you'd tell me."

"Why? Why would you want to get involved in any of this? It'll only lead to trouble, and a lot more than you can understand right now. Besides, I thought you had an important appointment, remember?" He tried to lighten the subject for a moment.

"Oh, that was for a job at the bank, but it can wait. I'd still like you to tell me what this is all about," Jennifer replied.

"Would you like to know about it if I told you your uncle had a part in it?" He stopped, looking down at her.

"My uncle?"

"Yes, and some other people too I'm not even sure of yet. But there were others, there had to be."

"I still want to know why all this happened," she continued.

"All right, then. But not around here. If you want to hear the whole story, let's get out of town someplace, maybe up to my old ranch at Quiet Creek. You willing to go that far?"

Nearly an hour later they came out on an open hillside above the abandoned buildings below. They walked down to the edge where they could sit on fresh spring grass and talk. Slowly, over the next half hour, he told her the entire story. She sat in rapt attention until he was finished.

"You really believe my uncle did that?" Jennifer finally asked.

"All I want is my place back. That's what I came back here for and that's what I'm going to do. And yes, I think Slaughter had a lot to do with me getting sent down to territorial prison, even though I can't prove it right now."

"It's just so hard to believe. I mean I know he's hardheaded, but the things you're talking about, why that even includes murder." She shook her head, still not wanting to think it might be so.

"Those men who called themselves bounty hunters tried to kill all three of us on Main Street that day. I saw Hollister down the block, and he didn't make a move to stop them or interfere in any way. Someone brought them here. They didn't just come riding in on their own, and those so-called 'papers' they were supposed to have on us never came up during my trial either, if there were any at all. All this was meant to drive us off Quiet Creek, but I still don't know why. I fought with your uncle from the day I started cutting timber for the cabin, and when he found out he couldn't run me off, I believe that's when he stooped to other means, and Hollister and maybe that deputy of his are in on it too. Now you know why I told you not to tell your uncle about that runaway buggy ride of yours."

Jennifer reached out slowly and touched Raffe's shoulder as he stared down at the weathered gray buildings.

"If I can help in any way I will. I don't know how, but I promise you I will."

Raffe turned to look at her.

"The best thing you can do is stay clear of all this. I only told you what happened because you asked, not because I expect you to try and help me. There's nothing you can do but get yourself in a whole lot of trouble, because it's going to get worse before it gets any better, and someone else might get killed over it. Four men have already died, and two of them were my brothers. I haven't forgotten that, and someone is going to pay."

Chapter Four

Cyrus Slaughter

That night at the Slaughter ranch, Jennifer sat at the big dinner table with her aunt Martha, her uncle, and ranch foreman Joe Cheek, who was only invited to eat occasionally when there was something important that Slaughter wanted to discuss with him. For the moment, the attention was focused on Jennifer.

"Well, how did the job interview go with Eaverhardt today?" her uncle asked, as Jennifer passed hot biscuits around the table.

"Oh, I got . . . held up and didn't get to see him in time. Maybe tomorrow I'll get an earlier start."

"You be sure you do, because I gave him a straight talking-to, and you've as good as got the job if you want it!" he snapped, pointing at a platter with his knife. "Pass me that beefsteak too, would you."

"You get rid of them nesters up on Big Meadow yet?" Slaughter continued, casting a scowl at Cheek.

"Me and the boys rode up there yesterday morning and told 'em to pack up their stuff and get going while they still could, like you said. They got one hardheaded plow boy named Ben Altman who keeps them together. We convinced him it ain't healthy to stick around and the rest will move out. We been puttin' the heat on 'em every time we get the chance. I heard some of their dry goods 'disappeared' one night, and they even had a fire that nearly burned a couple of wagons to the ground." Cheek smiled through unshaven whiskers.

"Well, you better get them outta there pretty quick, because if you don't I'll have to have . . . someone come in and do it for you. That's what I'm payin' you and the men for, not to have to go out and hire someone to do your job. And now that Latimer is back trying to make trouble again, it looks like we're going to have our hands full."

The old man took a long pull at the wine glass and glanced at the women, anxious for them to finish eating so he could go into more detail with Cheek once they were out of the room.

"You ladies about done yet?"

"Yes, Cyrus, we're done." Martha got to her feet and started to pick up the empty plates. "Come on, Jennifer, I know when your uncle wants to be left alone so he can have his man talk. We'll have our dessert in the kitchen."

"Wait a moment please, Aunt Martha. Uncle, when I was in town this morning, there was talk about Mr. Latimer and his ranch up on Quiet Creek. The sheriff even tried to have him jailed over nothing, just for being there. I heard that he had a right to homestead that ground. . . . is that true?"

Slaughter's eyes fell on his lovely niece and his face reddened, wondering why she would even ask such a question in the first place, and especially around the dinner table in front of everyone? He took in a long breath trying to control himself before answering then leaned forward.

"Let me tell you something young lady, something you obviously know nothing about, or you wouldn't ask in the first place. When I came to this country there wasn't any homestead law, and no squattin' on land someone else fought to keep with their own two hands. I took this ground with the few men I had and

I kept it against Indians, rustlers, prospectors, and anyone else who thought they could come in here and just take a piece of it, and I've held it for nearly forty years now. I didn't go 'ask' anyone if it was all right, and I didn't go sign any papers. This land was wild, wide open, and raw. No one on it except them savages. Do you think I'm going to let a wagon load of farmers, or someone like this Latimer come in here and start carving up what's mine and has been mine all these years because some two-bit politician in Washington thinks it's a good idea to pass a homestead act? This house you're living in and the food on this table that we're eating came from the land—my land—and no one is ever going to change that so long as I live and breathe! Now, I'm done talkin' about it, if you women will excuse us. I want to talk to Joe, here."

The next morning the old man had a horse saddled, and rode out with Cheek and several men to confront the wagoneers personally. First, they stopped on the hill overlooking the camp below. Smoke rose from a large campfire and the sound of axes rang off the trees surrounding the wagons.

"What in the world are they doing?" Slaughter cocked his head, standing in the stirrups, as

Cheek squinted into the morning sun without answering. They started down.

When they Entered the circle of wagons, several of the homesteaders came up to block further progress.

"What do you want here?" one asked, glaring at the riders.

"What do I want? Nothing from you sodbusters! I rode up here to tell you for the last time to get off my place. There ain't gonna be a next time. I let you squat on here for a couple of weeks, and now I want you to pack up and get out," Slaughter answered.

The chopping stopped and several men came out of the trees. Cyrus could see now that they were building a large log cabin back in the trees.

"You ain't building no cabin, not on my land, or anything else. I'm tellin' you right now, you either start outta here in the morning, or you're gonna wish you had!"

A tall man pushed his way through, ax still in hand as he came up to face the old man.

"You Slaughter?" he asked.

"That's right, I am. And who are you?"

"My name's Altman. I brought these people back all the way from Tennessee. Your men here have been trying to run us out since the first day we stopped here, but it isn't going to work. We've got as much right to settle on this land as anyone else with the homestead act now in place, and no one is going to stop us. Why don't you tell this bunch to back off before someone really gets hurt. If I have to, I'll go get the law to keep what we've got."

Cyrus leaned forward in the saddle, his face flushed red.

"You listen to me, you poppin' jay. You're on my ground, and I'm tellin' you and the rest of your sorry bunch to get off while you still can. I don't care if you go get the sheriff, the governor, or the president of the United States! This is your last warning. You stay, you're gonna wish you hadn't, and I won't be responsible for what happens. Now remember what I said. C'mon boys!"

As they pulled their horses around, Altman walked alongside the old man's horse and looked up at him.

"You send anymore men back here to harass us, and I'll get the law, like I said. I know that sheriff back in town is in your back pocket, but I'll get a lawman who isn't like a U.S. Marshal. You can mark my word on it."

Slaughter glanced over at Cheek and nodded quickly. The foreman gave out a sudden yell, and the riders spurred their animals between the wagons, scattering people, kicking over boxes, and spilling cooking pots into the fire as they thundered through. Up on top of the hill they looked back for a moment laughing, then turned and started for the ranch.

"We sure scared 'em, didn't we?" Cheek shouted over to Slaughter as they rode back.

"Yes, indeed" Slaughter answered, and grinned.

Jennifer Mitchell sat across the desk from the bank president Horace Earnhardt, answering questions.

"You say you took a secretarial course in college back east, is that correct, Miss Mitchell?"

"Yes, I did, and I've also had some experience in book-keeping too." She smiled.

"Well, I am looking for a woman willing to work and learn. Mrs. Deavons is leaving in two weeks, and I'll need someone to take her place who can take dictation, file records properly, and possibly even work a teller window and handle money when we get rushed a bit. You seem to have the qualifications—when could you start?"

"I'm ready whenever you want me, Mr. Earnhardt."

"All right then, let's see you here tomorrow

morning at eight o'clock, and I'll have Mrs. Deavons get you started. We don't open until nine-thirty, but it takes at least an hour to set up before I unlock the doors."

"Thank you, Mr. Earnhardt." She reached across the desk to shake his hand, catching him by surprise. "I'll do my best to take Mrs. Deavons' place."

As she headed for the door he couldn't help but take one more look at the stunning young redhead, knowing her looks alone would be an asset to the bank's business, not to mention her presence around him. He'd been a bachelor for a long time, and even though he was at least twice her age, who could tell what the future might hold for one of the most prosperous men in Placer City, and what he could offer a young woman who might be looking for position, security, and anything else money could buy. The more he thought about it, the more he was convinced that it didn't sound so far-fetched after all.

On the way back to her uncle's ranch, Jennifer pulled the buggy to a stop at the fork leading to Quiet Creek Ranch, tall weeds nearly obscuring the old, unused wheel track. She wondered if the tall man was back there somewhere, and suddenly decided to see for herself. She urged the horse forward for the next mile, going through a stand of dark woods, then breaking out into the open on the hillside above the abandoned buildings. When she stepped down and walked to the edge it seemed deserted, no horse tied to the old hitching post out front, and no one in sight. She decided to ride down anyway and see the place up close for herself.

When she stepped down and began surveying the buildings, she instantly felt an eerie stillness hanging over the place. Nothing stirred save the whisper of a soft breeze moving through empty windows and half-open doors. A rusted weathervane atop the barn creaked softly, trying to turn. She stepped up on the porch and pushed the door full open, peering into the shadowed interior. For a moment longer she did not enter, almost afraid of she didn't know what, then stepped inside, still feeling some kind of invisible presence.

"Raffe . . . Mr. Latimer . . . is anyone here?" she called softly, but got no answer. Her eyes slowly grew used to the dim light flooding through the windows, and she walked to the center of the big living room.

She stood before the huge stone fireplace, wondering how many cold winter evenings it had roared to life, warming the big ranch house with its cheery glow and snapping flames, only to stand empty and cold now. After several moments, she slowly walked down a darker hall leading to the back bedrooms, the musty smell of neglect growing stronger as she went, until finally she stood looking into the master bedroom, its wall hung with thick cobwebs. For some reason a cold chill ran up her spine, and she quickly retreated back into the living room and then out into the kitchen, its back door swung half open, revealing the big green meadow out back lit by brilliant sunlight. She went to the door and walked through, studying the dark trees sloping down the far side of the hill several hundred yards away. The warm sun and soft breeze felt good, and for several minutes she just stood there, taking in the scene and looking around at the out buildings behind the ranch house and the pole corral where Latimer once broke his horses. But, with the place abandoned, it was time to go. She turned and started back through the house, walking briskly into the living room. Suddenly, the dark form of a man blocked her way, and she made a small sound of fear, catching her breath as she tried to back away, her hands going to her face.

"I didn't mean to startle you, but I wasn't sure who it was." Raffe's familiar voice finally calmed her fear, as she let out a breath.

"You scared me for just a moment there!" She finally got the words out, still fighting to catch her breath. I never knew a man could walk so quietly."

"I'm sorry, Miss Mitchell. It's something you learn in prison when you don't want the guards to know you're moving around in the middle of the night in your cell."

"I didn't see your horse—how did you get out here?"

"He's tied back in the woods up on the hill. I didn't want anyone to know I was here. I took a walk across the meadow over to the creek, then upstream a ways, because I noticed it was muddy. At first I thought it was just spring run-off from the snow melt, but it was too dirty even for that, so I kept on going. You know what I found?"

"What?" she asked, her curiosity piqued.

"A half mile up around the bend a portion of the stream has been diverted and four big sluice boxes set in the riverbed. Someone is working it for gold, and from the looks of it, it's been going on for some time. Now I know why I was framed and sent to prison. Someone discovered gold on my place and decided to get rid of me one way or the other so they could get their hands on my ranch."

"But who, who's they?" Jennifer asked.

"I'd say Hollister, maybe that deputy of his, and your uncle. There could be others too. No one would put out that kind of labor unless they're taking out some real color. Now all I have to do is find out who's working those sluice boxes, or who's paying them."

"Raffe—I took a job in town at the bank. Maybe there's something I can find in their files about who bought your ranch."

"I already know who bought it; it was your uncle. That's what I was doing in town the other day when I ran into Hollister."

"My uncle!"

"That's right."

"Then I'll try to find out what he paid for it, and who else might be in on it," Jennifer replied.

"You remember when I told you not to get involved in this mess? Now you know why. You'll just get in deeper and you won't like what you find when you do, and I can tell you that right now." Raffe looked her square in the eye.

"I can't believe it—this whole thing—the murders of your brothers, you getting sent to prison and losing your ranch. Even if my uncle had a hand in it I want to help. You know no one else is going to, don't you? You've got just about everyone in town of importance dead set against you. I may be in a real position to help you once I start work."

Raffe put his hand lightly on Jennifer's back as he walked her outside to the buggy.

"Why do you want to do all this? You know you could be going against your own blood kin, don't you? Remember, that's your mother's brother we're talking about. Do you really think you could do that? It's not as easy as it sounds."

"I know it isn't. But if you're right, and I believe you are now, then this whole thing has been a terrible miscarriage of justice, and it needs to be made right so you can get your place back and clear your name."

"So, you mean to set it straight because of the law and nothing else, is that right?" He stepped closer to the buggy.

Jennifer's face flushed slightly as Raffe pressed her for an answer, and she hesitated, trying to come up with something plausible.

"Well . . . yes, that, and I'd like to be your . . . friend, to help you after what you did for me with the runaway horse . . . I guess that's part of it too."

He stood so close now that when she looked up into his eyes she could feel his breath on her face. For just an instant she had the urge to reach up and kiss him hard on the mouth, but she fought it back, picked up the buggy whip, and turned away.

"I've got to get back to the ranch now. Where are you going to be staying when I want to reach you?" she asked.

"I sure can't stay in town, so I've begun using an old hunting camp about five miles from here that my brothers and I set up in the mountains. No one will find me out there, but I don't want you having to go way out there, so why don't we meet here once or twice a week?"

"All right. I'll come every Tuesday and Friday after work. What are you going to do in the meantime?"

"I'm going to find out who's working those sluice boxes. You'd better get going now. By the way, do you mind if I call you Jennifer instead of Miss Mitchell?"

"I've been waiting for you to drop the formalities." She smiled, then slapped the reins across the horses' backs, and the buggy rattled away.

When Jennifer arrived at the ranch, Bart Hollister was just leaving. He did not stop and only tipped his hat lightly, riding by with a terse, "Miss Mitchell."

Slaughter was standing on the porch of the rambling ranch house, hands on his hips, as she stepped down. He was obviously infuriated about something.

"Hello, Uncle," Jennifer started to greet him. Instead of answering, he exploded.

"What in tarnation are you doing bailing that rascal Latimer out of jail! Don't you know any better than that? And why are you trying to help the likes of him anyway? I told you before he was nothing but trouble, didn't I? Bart just told me all about it, and at first I called him a damn liar! Don't you know you're going against your own kin, your own flesh and blood? Have you lost your mind, or some-thin'?"

She hesitated a moment, taken back by the ferocity of his remarks and fighting her own emotions, then decided to confront him.

"Yes, Uncle, I helped him out. That sheriff and his deputy put shotguns on him for abso-lutely no reason whatsoever, and if no one had been around they would have probably killed him just like they did his brothers, and for what! What do they know that's so bad they're willing to kill to keep it a secret, and maybe there's other people who know it too, and that's why they had him sent to prison. Do you know anything about it Uncle Cyrus? He told me you bought up his place when they sent him away. Is he right—did you really do that?"

Suddenly the old man advanced across the porch toward her in a rage, raising his hand. At that moment, Martha stepped through the front door and ran, wide-eyed, to stop him.

"Cyrus! Stop this minute. What are you doing? Have you lost your mind?" she screamed, grabbing his arm and slowly pulling it down as his eyes burned with hate.

"No, I haven't lost my mind . . . but I have lost a niece! If that's the thanks I get for taking her in like she was my own daughter, then it's time she went someplace else to live, not here, not under my roof. I'm done with you; you're not part of this family anymore!"

Jennifer stood stunned, hardly believing what she'd just heard. Martha pleaded with Slaughter to change his mind, but he would not.

"That's all right, Aunt. I'll pack my things and move into town. Please, don't beg him anymore, and don't cry. Maybe it's all for the best after all."

She turned and hurried past the old man, then upstairs to pack her things. When she came down later her aunt still stood on the porch weeping softly in despair, wiping her eyes.

"I'm . . . so sorry dear . . . I'm sure he'll

change his mind once he calms down and I can talk to him."

"Don't, Aunt Martha, it'll only make it harder for you here. I'll be all right. I've got a job now and can find a place to stay. When you get to town, please come visit me. I'll miss you, you know that. I'm sorry it's come to this, but there's something bigger behind it all, and I've got to find out what that is. Good-bye for now."

"I've asked one of the hands to take you to town in the buggy. I wish someone would tell me what this is all about."

"I can't, Aunt Martha, but maybe in time it will all come out. Promise me you'll take care of yourself."

She kissed her aunt lightly on the cheek, then lifted her bags in the buggy and got in. A moment later, the buggy started away from the ranch, leaving Martha Slaughter confused and weeping again as it went out of sight.

The next morning Latimer left the hidden camp and rode several miles until he neared Quiet Creek. He then tied off his horse and started down through thick woods, packing his Winchester. Farther down the steep slope he heard voices above rushing water, and crouching, he advanced further until he could see half a dozen men working steadily at the sluice boxes. As he watched, three riders came down the trail alongside the creek. He instantly recognized old man Slaughter as one of them.

They dismounted and went to the nearest box, while Slaughter gestured toward a gold pan. One of the men picked it up, then scooped out the pebbles and black sand at the end of the box, and kneeled to wash it out. In a few moments he was done, and the men gathered around to finger the results, smiling and patting each other on the back. Now Raffe knew for sure what he'd suspected. Slaughter must have helped frame him to get his ranch for the gold. He slid down a few more yards, trying to hear what they were talking about, when his foot suddenly dislodged a big rock hidden under the mat of slippery pine needles, sending it tumbling end over end until it careened into the creek with a resounding splash. Instantly all the men lifted their eyes to scan the dark trees above them, and several men ran for their rifles.

"Who's up there?" they shouted, as Raffe scrambled back uphill as fast as his legs would carry him. The excited yells from below grew louder.

"There he goes . . . shoot quick . . . don't let him get away!"

The whine and crack of bullets splintering tree trunks kept him dodging and ducking until he finally reached the top and quickly mounted up and rode away, leaving his pursuers far below.

Two days later, he waited at the old ranch for Jennifer to meet him. When she did not show, he went back to camp wondering what had happened. Late the very next afternoon he took the chance of riding into town. He then watched from a shadowed doorway, hat pulled low, while Jennifer and the other employees came out after work and she headed for the tiny apartment she'd rented one block off of Main Street. No sooner had she entered and locked the door than he quickly knocked. She asked who was there without opening the door.

"It's me, Raffe." He kept his voice low, looking back over his shoulder to be sure no one was around. Jennifer quickly unlocked the door and pulled him inside, instantly wrapping her arms around him in relief as he stood, surprised by the sudden show of emotion. Then he gently pulled her even closer.

"What's the matter, why are you staying here in town? When you didn't show at the ranch I decided to come looking for . . ."

"Oh Raffe, I'm so glad to see you. My uncle ordered me off the ranch after the sheriff told him I bailed you out of jail. I had to find a place to stay so I took this place, but I didn't have any way to meet you yesterday. I knew you'd wonder what happened to me and hoped you'd come looking for me even though it's dangerous for you."

Over the next hour, he told her all about the gold dredging operation and Slaughter's appearance there, and she explained that she hadn't been able to get into the land records yet but was still trying. Suddenly, there was a knock on the door. Jennifer quickly ushered him behind a curtained partition that served as a bedroom, then went to answer it.

"Who is it?" she called, without opening the door.

"Ahhhh, Miss Mitchell, it's me . . . Horace Eaverhardt . . . from the bank? I was wondering if you'd care to . . . would you open the door so I can talk to you?"

She cracked it open just far enough so that their eyes met. The nervous little man fingered the brim of his hat in his hand and forced a weak smile.

"I know this is, well, highly unusual, but I just found out today that . . . errrr . . . maybe I should say you left your uncle's ranch to move into town, and I was wondering . . . well, if you haven't had dinner yet I'm on my way to dine at the Charlton House. They serve the finest dinner in town, and I was just wondering if you'd care to eat with . . . me?"

"I'm sorry, Mr. Eaverhardt, but I just don't feel like going out tonight. We had a long day at the bank, and I want to stay here and retire early. I'm really not hungry at all. I'm sure you understand?"

"Why, of course I do . . . I just thought you might want some . . . company, being all alone and such. I mean sociable company of course, nothing more. It's just down the street you know . . . not far?"

"No thank you, I'm staying in tonight, but I'll see you in the morning. Now, you'll have to please excuse me, but thank you for asking and good night."

She slowly began closing the door while Eaverhardt continued to try to convince her, his face growing red with embarrassment. Finally, after they were sure he'd left, Raffe came back out, smiling quickly at her.

"Looks like you've already got yourself an admirer."

"He's made a few strange remarks, but I won't let it go any further. I need this job if I'm going to keep this place, but I don't know what he's thinking."

"You don't? I do. You're young and attractive, and single. Any man in town would like to put an apron on you."

"Would they? Well, I'm not ready for that yet. Maybe later, but not now. Can I ask you something a bit personal?"

He nodded, wondering what was next.

"Does it . . . bother you, that someone, anyone might pay attention to me or ask me out?"

They were standing only feet away as he leveled his gaze at her without the slightest show of emotion, searching for the right thing to say and worried about how to say it. When the silence continued, she tried again.

"Well, does it, Raffe?"

He finally moved forward, encircling her with his arms. He kept his eyes on hers, their faces only inches apart.

"Okay. In a way it does, I guess. Is that what you wanted me to say?"

"Yes, it is."

She reached up on tiptoes and kissed him lightly on the lips, her slender hands around his neck.

"I've been here in Placer City long enough to know that you're very different from most other men. I also know that my uncle fears your presence, as does Sheriff Hollister. I don't think they'll stop at anything to get rid of you, Raffe, and that means you'll have to be very careful about coming to town. It makes me sick to think what Uncle Slaughter did, and I know my mother wouldn't believe her brother was capable of something like that. I'll try to rent a horse and ride out to the ranch the day after tomorrow after work. Will you meet me there?"

"Yes, I will, but just be sure you're not followed by anyone. You're in this up to your neck now—you know that, don't you? There's no turning back or telling what might happen or who might get hurt, and you're the last person I want to see any kind of harm come to, Jennifer. I guess by now that's pretty clear, isn't it?"

"Yes, it is. I think maybe I knew that from the very first day you stopped the buggy. Sometimes you just know there's something about someone that's special, and it's a connection that's almost impossible to put into words . . . you just know it."

Raffe cupped her slender face in his big, rough hands a moment longer without saying anything, then finally turned and opened the door, heading out into the night.

Chapter Five

Southern Riders

Jake McCannlis and his two sons, Elijah and Samuel, reined their horses to a stop at the top of the hill overlooking Placer City. The boys cast sideways glances at their father's bewhiskered face and waited for orders.

"Well, you think he's here, Paw?" Elijah, the oldest of the pair finally asked, as McCannlis squinted through bushy eyebrows at the buildings scattered below.

"Me'be, me'be not, but we'll ride down and find out, and you two keep yer trap shut when we get there, understand? I'll do all the talkin'."

"What about the law, if they got any?" Samuel finally spoke up. "A town that big sure enough must have a lawman in it, don't you think?"

"We got all the law we need right here in my saddlebags. The Good Book tells us what we have ta' do!" Jake patted the leather containers behind him and, shifting the rifle across his lap, spat a stream of dark, brown tobacco juice. "Vengeance is mine, sayeth the Lord, and by God that's exactly what I mean to do when I catch up to Latimer for what he done to Orrin! Now, let's git down there, and remember what I said."

When the ragtag threesome rode down Main Street, passersby stared and whispered to each other under their breath. At the end of the street, they stepped down in front of the Double Eagle Saloon, and went inside, where Clint Richie and several friends were already seated at a table near the window.

"Would you get a load of them three," one of Richie's friends growled as the men came in and went up to the bar, the old man pausing to look around the half-empty room.

"What'll it be boys?"

The bartender came up, winking beyond the three to the deputy and his friends.

"We don't hold with no whiskey drinkin'. I

just came in here lookin' for somebody, me'be ask a few questions." Jake pursed his lips, staring at the barkeep.

"I don't sell answers, mister. This is a bar. If you want advice, the Methodist Church is down Main Street, then up the hill to the right about a block. Try there."

"You sorta got a smart mouth fer someone with so much grease in his hair!" McCannlis shot back, his short-fuse temper already burning.

"Lookit. I didn't ask you to come in here, so why don't you just head back out those doors the way you came in before you make any trouble for yourself and these two idiots you got with you. I'm running a bar, not a social club." His hands slowly went down until he could feel the cold, blue steel of the double-barrel shotgun hidden under the bar.

"All I wanna know is if there's a man around here named Raffe Latimer. I never seen 'im, and I don't know what he looks like. All I got is a name."

Richie quickly got to his feet and walked over, then leaned on the bar next to McCannlis.

"I'm the deputy sheriff here. I heard you say you were looking for Raffe Latimer, is that right? What business you got with him?"

The old man looked Richie up and down

scornfully before answering, then thought better of it, holding his tongue. He didn't want the law involved in this in any way, so he searched his mind for an excuse.

"I . . . heard of him down south, that's all, heard he came up into this part of the country . . . he owes me . . . some money, and I came to collect. You ain't got him locked up in jail, do ya?"

"No, but it's probably just a matter of time before we do. What's your name, anyway, and where are you from down south?"

"Name's Jake McCannlis, and this here is my two boys, Elijah and Samuel. We been ridin' pretty near three weeks to git here, and now I wanna find him."

"You plan on staying in town someplace?" Richie pressed.

"In town? Heck no. We ain't got no money for doin' that. We'll just fix us up a camp in timber fer now."

"Well, Sheriff Hollister just might want to talk to you about all this, so once you get settled in it would be a good idea if you ride in and drop by our office. It's down at the end of the block on the corner. I'll tell him to expect you."

McCannlis scowled at the predicament he'd walked right into. Richie's appearance and questions were bad enough, and now he'd brought the sheriff in on it too.

"Well . . . maybe I might show up," he grumbled, turning away.

"No maybe to it. I'll tell Hollister you're in town and what for. He's already on the prowl for Latimer, and he'll want to hear your story. You just be sure you stop by."

The old man glared at the boys, jerking his head toward the door. "Let's git on outta here," he ordered.

Richie watched them go, then called out just as they stepped outside. "Remember, we're down on the corner. Don't forget."

Once they were gone, his friends came up to the bar, laughing sarcastically about the trio.

"When's the last time you think any of them took a bath?" one said, elbowing the deputy.

"Yeah," commented another. "I've seen some pretty sorry-looking hicks in my time, but those three take the cake. I'll bet they could skin a cat faster than you could say 'go.' "

Richie wasn't laughing as he walked to the window and watched the three mount up and ride away, talking to himself as much as the others. "They're not here to collect no money. There's something else going between them three. Listen, I've got to get going. I want to find Hollister. I'll see you guys later."

* * *

Down at the bank, Jennifer was assigned to work a teller window for the first time. As she busied herself counting out the money in her drawer, she heard the front door open for the first customer. She didn't look up though, until she realized someone was standing directly in front of her window. When she looked up, she looked directly into the eyes of a strikingly handsome stranger with a quick smile, coal black hair, and a pencil line mustache. He was tipping his hat, his deep blue eyes riveted on her.

"Well, hello," he said smoothly, openly looking at what he could see of her not blocked by the countertop. "What's a pretty young thing like you doing working on a day like this? You ought to be out with a buggy, a picnic lunch, and a gentleman to escort you . . . say someone like me?"

His sudden boldness stopped her from commenting for a moment. Then she composed herself and answered. "Can I help you?" she replied, as he lifted several saddle-bags on top of the counter, pulling out several stacks of bills.

"Why yes, you surely can, both right here and after you get off of work. I want to open an account and deposit this money, then when you're done this afternoon, take you out to dinner. I'm new in town and don't know my way around, so you'll have to pick out the best place."

"I'm sorry, I can only help you with business transactions, Mr . . . ?" She looked at him quizzically.

"Quick, Johnny Quick. My friends just call my Johnny, and I want you to do the same. There's two thousand five hundred dollars here, Miss . . . Mrs . . . ?"

"I'm Jennifer Mitchell, Mr. Quick."

"No," he interrupted. "Johnny, remember?"

"If you'll just fill out this deposit slip I can open an account for you, Mr. Quick," She replied. A quick smile flashed across his face at her stubborn formality.

"Well, okay. Listen, Miss Mitchell." He leaned forward, talking almost under his breath. "I understand here in the bank you have to act this way, but when you get off of work you don't have to be so formal, do you? I don't care to eat alone, and I want you for company. That's just 'good business,' isn't it?"

"Are you going to fill out a deposit slip, or aren't you?" she persisted, until he finally grabbed the pen and began writing.

"Well, all right," he began, without looking up, "if you're going to be all business, then maybe you can tell me where I can find a man named Cyrus Slaughter. He's got a ranch someplace around here, doesn't he?"

Her breath caught in her throat at the mention of the name, and she stopped counting the money to look up at him.

"Cyrus Slaughter is my uncle." She looked quickly around the room behind her, hoping no one—especially Mr. Eaverhardt sitting at his desk in the corner—would hear or notice their prolonged conversation.

"His ranch is south of town, about an hour's ride. Do you mind if I ask you what business you have with him?"

"Your uncle? Well, how nice. That means we might be seeing each other after all, and no, I don't mind if you ask because it's just that, 'business,' and being a businesswoman yourself you understand why it's confidential, don't you?" He got in a little jab at her.

She stared at him a moment longer, then finished the paperwork and pushed it back across the marble counter toward him, asking him to sign it.

"Do we have a dinner invitation then?" he asked again.

"No, WE do not. Now would you please step aside so customers behind you can come up?"

He quickly scribbled his name, then tipped his hat and turned, starting for the door. Jennifer noticed his dapper, tailored suit, his fancy gun belt and holster, and his clean black boots. Johnny Quick was no saddle-riding cow puncher, that was for sure. There was something about his demeanor, something almost sinister and dangerous under that thin smile, like a fiddle string pulled taught and ready to snap at the slightest provocation. She'd never seen a gunfighter before, but he seemed to fit every description she'd ever heard of what one acted and looked like. What business could he possibly have with her Uncle Slaughter? Whatever it was, she had that prickly feeling that there would be trouble behind it. Big trouble.

When Quick rode up to the Slaughter ranch later that day, he was led into the old man's office, where Slaughter was working on papers. The old man looked up to study the thin man neatly dressed in a dark suit, and then nodded toward a chair opposite him.

"Drink?" he offered. Quick accepted, then both men touched glasses, eyeing each other over the sour mash.

"So, you're the man my friends down south told me about, huh?" Slaughter began. "I hear you don't work cheap, but do good work, is that right?"

"Anyone who works cheap is worth exactly what you pay for them. I do what others either don't or won't do, and that's never cheap, Mr. Slaughter. What is it you'd like done up here?" He smiled that thin, cold grin of his, and over the next hour the old man told him all about the nesters up at Big Meadow, and his unsuccessful efforts to force them out over the months.

"There's one they call Ben Altman, he's keeping them together. Get rid of him, and the whole bunch will pick up and leave."

"Okay. I want one of your men to show me around up there, but for today I'll just unpack my things. Where will I be staying?"

"Right here in the big house with me and my wife, Martha. I've got a spare bedroom in back where you can come and go as you please. I don't want you staying in the bunkhouse with the rest of the hands, not with what you're here for. That'll be just between you and me. Now, what's your fee for this job?"

"It's one thousand dollars in cash, no checks, no bank drafts. I guarantee my work, like I said before. You pay me now, before I have a little 'talk' with this Altman. That way there's no, shall we say 'problems,' collecting after I'm done. By the way, not to change the subject, but I ran into your niece at the bank today. She's the one who told me how to get out here. She's not married, is she?"

"Her name's Jennifer Mitchell, but we don't use that name around here anymore, and I'd appreciate it if you didn't either. She turned against me and her own aunt, and I told her to pack up and go."

"What did she do to bring that on?"

"Nothing I want to talk about, at least not now. Maybe later I'll have another job for you over it. Now, get your things and I'll show you your room. Later I'll have Joe Cheek, that's my foreman, show you the place."

That afternoon when Eaverhardt stepped out of the bank for a late lunch, Jennifer quickly went to the records room in the vault and began going through files looking for her uncle's papers. When she found them, there was nothing there about the purchase of Quiet Creek. For several moments she fought disappointment, then on a whim she pulled up the bank president's own papers, shuffling through them while looking over her shoulder to be sure she wasn't being watched. When she'd dug down nearly to the bottom of the stack, she suddenly came upon a deed to what had been Raffe's and his brothers' ranch. Her heartbeat quickened as she read the document. Quiet Creek had been purchased for a mere $1,500 in a three-way split between her uncle, Eaverhardt, and Bart Hollister! Raffe had been right all along. They'd framed him to get his ranch and the gold they had discovered there in the creek.

Quickly, she put the papers back and closed the file drawer. She had to tell Raffe just as soon as possible. For the rest of that afternoon she kept thinking about the powerful ramifications of what she'd found. Now if there was just some way they could actually prove all this.

The next afternoon after work, she changed into riding clothes, then rented a horse from the livery stable and rode out to the ranch. When she came out of the trees overlooking the buildings, Raffe was waiting for her. She quickly explained what she'd discovered in the bank files, and he listened without interruption. When she finished, he reached out and put a gentle hand on her shoulder.

"Jennifer, you've found the answer to a question I had all the years I was behind bars. Now I've got to find some way to prove it in a court of law and get my ranch back, but that won't happen here in Placer City, not with your uncle, Hollister, and Richie against me. I've got to do it some other way. And there's another thing I'm going to need before I try. I hate to ask you to stick your neck out again after all you've done."

"What is it, Raffe? You know I'll do anything I can to help."

"I need those papers from the bank vault. They're the only legal documents that prove my story. Without them, it's just my word against those three, and if anyone gets wind of this they'll destroy them and say they've either been lost or misplaced. Maybe I could take them down to the circuit judge who comes through Granite Pass from time to time."

"I'll get them, but it might take me a few days" Jennifer replied. "I have to wait until Eaverhardt and the others are out to lunch and I've got the bank mostly to myself. Maybe I could even stay late one night if he'd let me. I could say I had to catch up on some book work."

"That's all up to you—just be careful, whatever you do. If you have to wait a little while don't worry about it. Just make sure the time is right and you don't get caught. I wish there was some other way." Raffe sighed.

"Well, there isn't, and besides, you know by now this is where I want to be, helping you clear your name and get back what's rightfully yours. Now, would you ride partway back to town with me? It'll be dark soon, and I don't want to ride alone."

His cool, steady gaze never left her face as she leaned over close and kissed him gently, her hands sinking into the long hair on the back of his neck.

The next morning, Joe Cheek and several hands rode out above the homesteader's camp, and Cheek explained the layout to Johnny Quick.

"There they are, the whole sorry bunch of 'em. You want us to ride down there and back you up?"

"No, you head back to the ranch. I'll take care of this myself."

"You sure? What if they decide to put up a fight? You can't take 'em all on."

"They won't. Go ahead back to the ranch. I'll be along later."

"You gonna kill 'em straight out? I'd sure like to stick around and see that!"

"Don't worry about it. Just get everybody out of here and leave it to me."

"Okay. But I hope you know what you're gettin' yourself into."

Cheek and the others pulled their horses around and started back, while Quick slowly descended the hillside, heading toward the circle of canvas-topped prairie schooners. When he reined his horses to a halt, several women watched him come in and called out to their men working on the cabin. The men quickly appeared as Quick dismounted and walked forward, studying the sweat-soaked men for a moment longer.

"Who are you, and what do you want?" one of the farmers demanded, taking a step forward.

"You Altman?" Quick asked.

"No. I am." A big man stepped through the crowd, an ax still in his hand, and sized up the dapper visitor.

"Good. I represent Cyrus Slaughter, the owner of this land you're squatting on. I'm here to tell you you've got until tomorrow morning to pack up all your gear and get out of here."

"Are you a lawman? You got papers saying we have to leave?"

"Yes, I'm a lawman of sorts. I enforce the law for various people who've been put upon when normal channels don't work, and this is one of those times. You've got until morning, so if I were you I'd start packing right now while you can."

"He's no lawman, Ben, he's a hired gun!"

One of the others pointed accusingly at Quick.

"Let me tell you something" Ben said. "Mr. Slaughter's tried to drive us off of here before. It didn't work then, and it won't work now. We've got as much right to settle here as anyone else does, and there's nothing you or anyone else can do to change it. Now go back and tell your boss it didn't work, because we aren't going to move one inch!"

"Well, that's not so." Quick stepped forward until he stood only feet away from the big man, staring him in the face with his cold blue eyes.

"What do you mean by that?" Altman asked. "Do you think you can scare us off?"

"No, I'm not trying to scare you off. . . . I'm going to kill you right where you stand, if you're still here when I return tomorrow."

"You do, and you'll hang for it!"

"You'll never know about it because you'll be in a pine box buried right here in this ground you've been trying to steal. Now, remember what I said because I won't say it again. You know what's coming. Either pack up or I'll drop you before the sun hits those wagons."

He turned and mounted up, looking down at the circle of men. Several women held their hands to their mouths, eyes wide in horror as he rode slowly away.

* * *

Back at the ranch, Slaughter and Cheek were standing on the porch watching him come in. When he got down and started up the steps, Slaughter popped the question.

"Well, what happened? Did you run 'em off?"

"They'll either be gone by morning, or Altman will be dead. Once I take him down that will be the end of it."

"Just like that? You think they're gonna turn tail and run for it that easy?"

"Trust me. It'll work. Altman's just like the rest of those farmers. He didn't push a wagon two thousand miles to die over a piece of ground he can't hold, and he knows it. If he does get his back up, then I'll settle it my way. He knows what I'll do to him, and one way or the other he'll be gone tomorrow."

"You're pretty darn cocksure of yourself, ain't you?" Slaughter's voice had a touch of sarcasm in it.

"I make it my business to know people, Mr. Slaughter. That's why I wanted to ride out and see him face to face. He's a dirt farmer, not a gunfighter. You see, as long as they can stick together as a group they have each other for support, but now that I've called him out, just him alone, that's all gone. Damn few men have ever actually pulled a weapon on another man and meant to kill him. I have. He hasn't, and neither have the rest of them. They're all law-abiding, God-fearing people. All sod-busters are like that. They live by the Good Book, so he's the only one I'll have to deal with. He doesn't stand a chance, and he knows it. Now, all this riding and talking has made me thirsty. Why don't we go inside and have something to drink?"

The next morning at breakfast Quick took his time eating while Cyrus watched him out of the corner of his eye, growing more impatient by the minute, until he couldn't stand it any longer.

"Well, when are you headin' out for Big Meadow?"

"Soon as I'm done eating and have had another cup of coffee. Stop worrying about it. They're leaving, just like I said."

"I still think you ought to take some of my men with you just in case any of the rest of 'em try to make trouble."

"No, I won't need them. Just let me handle this my way. That's what you're paying me one thousand dollars for, remember? You just keep that town sheriff off my back, and everything will be all right."

"You don't have to worry about him none. He's one of us, and besides, he knows what side his bread is buttered on. I just want them damn farmers off my land once and for all!"

Later, when Quick rode down toward the camp, he saw a knot of men standing outside the wagons. Several shouted a warning as he came up and dismounted. He looked around for Altman, who appeared out of the crowd. Johnny carefully eased his riding coat back to clear his gun belt and pistol, then walked straight toward the big man, stopping just fifteen feet away.

"I'm not armed!" Altman called out. "You can't pull on an unarmed man. That's murder no matter how you call it."

"Either get a gun or get up on that wagon and get out of here."

"I ain't no gun fighter, and I won't get a weapon," Altman insisted.

"I won't tell you again. Get up on that seat now, or I'll drop you where you stand!"

"I won't fight you, you're . . ."

In an instant Johnny drew and fired. The .45-caliber slug drove Altman backwards onto the ground, where he rolled around in pain and cried out. The others ran back and women shrieked in terror. Smoothly, Quick leapt over the top of the wounded man, pistol pointing straight down at his face as the big man clutched his stomach with both hands and the growing blossom of bloody red stained his shirt.

"Don't . . . shoot again!" Altman cried out, as Johnny cocked the hammer back deliberately, then looked around at the others.

"Put him in a wagon and all of you get out of here or I'll put the next one through his head!"

"Don't do it, we'll load him up—we'll leave, just let him live!" one of the men shouted, then several ran up to drag the wounded man back toward the wagons. Johnny stayed put, gun in hand, watching the commotion and prodding them on.

Forty minutes later the first wagons rattled forward, then started across the far end of Big Meadow as the farmers whipped their teams on one after another. Finally the last one disappeared out of sight behind the trees and everything grew quiet and still again, save the crackling pop of flames and column of dark smoke spiraling up from the half-finished cabin, as Johnny Quick stood and watched it burn.

Chapter Six

The Payoff

Quick returned to the ranch with news he'd finally driven the squatters off once and for all. Old man Slaughter was nearly dumbfounded that one man could actually accomplish what he and all his men could not after months of intimidation and vandalism.

"You dead sure they're gone?" he asked, as a hard quick smile spread over Johnny's face.

"I said so, didn't I?"

Slaughter got up and called Cheek into his office.

"I want you to ride up to Big Meadow and tell me if those sodbusters are still there or not, then get back here."

"Okay, boss." The foreman turned on his heel and left the office.

Slaughter poured two drinks, then sat back down in his big leather chair and studied his hired gunfighter thoughtfully as he sipped at the sour mash.

"You know, I was just thinking, I might be able to use a man like you for maybe another month or so."

"No, Mr. Slaughter, this ranching isn't for me." Quick replied. "I'm a business man, not a cow puncher. After you pay my fee I'm riding into town to get me a room at the Double Eagle for a few days. I might do a little gambling, and visit a certain young lady who's caught my eye, but that's about it. I'll leave the cattle, the flies, and the smell to your men here. It's not my game and never has been. Besides, I've never liked working that hard or staying in one place that long either. You get too many attachments, and that can make you careless. In my business that's something I won't let happen, so I'll just stick around long enough to see how my poker luck is running, and pick up a few dollars while I'm enjoying myself."

"You'll be passing up some easy money if you do," Cyrus tried one more time.

"I don't think so. Easy money is sitting with four aces and enough chips in front of you to clean the table. It can even be better than pulling one of my Colts. After your foreman gets back I'll go change and pack my bags. Just be sure you've got my money ready."

Later, when Cheek returned to verify that the homesteaders had, indeed, abandoned their camp, Slaughter called Quick back into the office and pushed a wrapped stack of bills across the desk at him.

"Well, there's your money. I suppose you want to count it?"

"Yes, I do." Quick picked it up and thumbed quickly through the bills. "It's correct, and it's been nice doing business with you, Mr. Slaughter." He reached out and shook the old man's hand, then the three men walked out onto the front porch.

"Remember what I said." Slaughter growled. "I could still use a man of your 'talents' for some other work I might need shortly."

"That will have to be for another day. By the way, thank your wife for her hospitality and the fine meals she served up. Now I want to get going."

As Quick rode away, Slaughter turned to Cheek and spoke under his breath.

"There's an odd duck for you. But I'll give

him this, he knows how to handle those six-guns he's packing. He sure put the run on them farmers when we couldn't. It was worth a thousand just to get 'em the hell off my place."

When Quick got to town, he rented a room upstairs at the Double Eagle, then walked down to the corner to the bank to deposit the lion's share of his money from Slaughter, holding out enough for gambling and hotel bills. Once again he tried to engage Jennifer in conversation to ask her out. Again she resisted his efforts and kept their brief talk focused on his banking business. Just as he was ready to leave, he tried one last ploy.

"You know, if you keep turning me down like this I might just have to stay here in Placer City longer than I expected until you agree."

"You can stay or go as you please, Mr. Quick. Your business is something for you to worry about, not me. Now thank you, and good day."

He stepped back from the counter, still staring at her, a thin smile flashing across his face as he tipped his hat, then finally turned for the door.

Raffe had decided to stay in town secluded at Jennifer's apartment in case she could get into the vault room and retrieve the deed papers. After she rushed home during lunch hour without success, he grew restless and decided to try going out later that afternoon. He pulled his hat low across his face and moved down the boardwalk along Main Street, heading for the hardware store to buy some extra cartridges. The town had changed a lot in five years, and most of the people out that afternoon didn't know who he was or where he'd been all that time, until he pushed through the door of Layton's Hardware and Dry Goods store. Owner Homer Layton recognized him instantly when he walked in.

"Why, Raffe—Raffe Latimer! For goodness sake, I didn't know you were back in town again. When did you get in, how are you after . . . after . . . being gone so long? Let me take a look at you. You know, Raffe, some of us here thought you got a pretty raw deal over those shootings. Not everyone sided with Hollister and his bunch, not by a long shot."

As the two men greeted each other, two aisles over, behind a row of hanging pots and pans, Jake McCannlis and his sons instantly stopped what they were doing and leaned low, peering through the utensils at the big man they had ridden so far to find and kill. After a moment, McCannlis pushed Samuel and Elijah out the door, glancing over his shoulder. They stepped quickly into an afternoon sun casting long shadows across the street. McCannlis looked around, then gave them orders.

"We'll step into this alley right here until he comes out, then let him pass. Once he does, we'll step out and shoot 'im down like the dog he is, just like he did Orrin!" McCannlis' little eyes burned bright with hate.

"Ain't we gonna call 'im out first?" Elijah asked.

"Did he give your brother a chance when he shot him down, you idiot?" McCannlis's voice rose nearly to a shout. "Don't you think about nothin' except what I tell you ta' do. Soon as he passes us, walk out and empty them pistols of yours in 'im. Then we'll run for our horses before anyone knows what happened or who did it. Now get them guns outta your waist-bands and be ready."

Raffe stayed in Layton's another few minutes talking, then finally picked up his package and shook hands with Layton.

"I'm real glad you're back, Raffe, and I know a lot of other people are too. You stop by anytime you're in town, whether you need anything or not. You're always welcome here."

Raffe thanked Layton, then headed for the door, pausing for just a moment as he stepped outside. He looked up and down the street, then started down the boardwalk, not noticing the three shadowy figures crouched in the alley as he went past. At that same moment Johnny Quick exited the bank and started back to the Double Eagle. The long shafts of setting sun illuminated the big man as he strode by across the street. Just as Quick smiled and started to call out Raffe's name, he saw three men rush out of the alley behind Raffe with guns leveled straight at him. He shouted a warning.

"Preacher, look out!"

Raffe reacted instantly, knowing only one man would call him that name. He turned and crouched, dropping his package and pulling out his .45. A volley of crashing shots suddenly filled the quiet streets like bogus thunder, and passersby dove for cover. Quick's pistol shot flames and lead, cutting McCannlis down face first onto the mud-caked walkway. His boys backpedaled and continued to fire, until Elijah went down with a pair of bullets in his chest. Samuel turned to run, but Quick dropped him before he could reach the alley.

When the haze of blue gun smoke cleared, both men straightened up. They looked across at each other as people flooded back out onto the street, circling the three dead men, then crowding around Raffe and Quick as they came together.

"You sure know how to attract trouble, don't you?" Quick commented, glancing behind Raffe to the McCannlis men.

"Looks like it, but I don't even know who they are. I've never seen any of them before."

Raffe pushed old man McCannlis over with his boot, staring down at his blood-stained, whiskered face.

"What about the other two—you sure you haven't seen them someplace before? They sure seemed to know you."

They walked over, looking at the two young men, while Raffe shook his head again.

"Nope, but it's a good thing you came along when you did. I owe you one for that."

"You don't owe me anything, preacher. We'll just call it square for those beans and lousy coffee you fixed me that night on the trail, remember?" Quick reloaded his six-gun, smiling up at Raffe with that strange grin of his.

Just then, Jennifer burst through the crowd of people surrounding them and threw her arms around Raffe. Her hand felt something warm and wet on his shirtsleeve, and she pulled back, carefully straightening his arm.

"Raffe, you're hurt. Your shirt's bloody . . . Let's get you over to the doctor right now!"

Quick took a step back, staring at the two of them incredulously.

"You mean you know her?" His eyes showed genuine surprise, as Jennifer pulled herself close against Raffe's chest, trying to control her emotions.

"Yes, we're . . . friends."

"Friends? Well, I'll be darned!"

At that moment, Hollister and Richie came running up, guns drawn, quickly checking out the three dead men, then pushing through the crowd and leveling their guns at Latimer.

"That's it. Throw down your gun and un-buckle that belt!" Hollister ordered. Raffe didn't make a move to comply and as the two men faced each other, Quick walked to his side, ready for anything else that might happen.

"Just wait a minute . . . What's your name, sheriff?" Quick asked. "I saw the whole thing from right over there. Those three dirt-bags tried to bushwhack preacher here from behind that alley. If I hadn't seen them and yelled to him he'd be dead—shot—instead of the other way around. He never drew and fired until I yelled, and you've got my word on that."

"Your word!" Hollister almost laughed out

loud. "And who in the heck are you, that 'your word' means anything to me or anyone else around here?"

Quick introduced himself, then pointed at Richie.

"You better tell that 'boy' of yours to holster that gun before he gets any more nervous than he already is, and he pulls one off accidentally."

Hollister turned to the deputy and ordered him to put his gun away, then looked back at Quick and Latimer.

"Like I said, he fired in self-defense, and if I have to tell it to a court of law, I'll be around here long enough to do so. There's a street full of witnesses to back it up."

"You will, huh? Well, mister, I've never seen you before, so your word around here isn't worth the paper it's written on, as far as I'm concerned. What are you doing in Placer City? Do you have a job—work at anything— or are you just another fancy-dressed drifter looking for trouble?

Quick felt a tremor of anger rush through him, and he had the urge to call out Hollister then and there, but he fought it back, knowing that the sheriff was trying to pin something on Raffe any way he could. Instead, he took in a slow breath, then finally answered.

"I've just completed some 'business' for the Slaughter ranch. You know him? He owns half the country around here."

Instantly, Hollister's face changed from contempt to surprise. He looked Quick up and down, then glanced over at Richie.

"Yeah, I know him, and I want you two to come down to my office to straighten this shooting out right now. Let's go!"

"I'm going too," Jennifer insisted. "But first, Raffe has to see a doctor." Hollister started to argue, then let it go as he hustled them up the street toward Doc Wells' place. Later, after half an hour of haranguing threats, the three finally left the sheriff's office and moved back out into the darkened streets.

"This two-bit sheriff of yours doesn't think much of you, does he?" Quick smiled. "I bet he'd hang you in a minute if he had half the chance."

"It's a long story. Goes all the way back to before I was sent to prison." Raffe didn't elaborate any further.

"Well, I'm free for the evening now that you didn't get us thrown in jail, so I'd say it's time for dinner. Why don't you two join me? Besides, I want to know what you've been doing since the last time I saw you, considering three men just tried to kill you. You must be doing something someone doesn't like, right, preacher?"

"Preacher?" Jennifer interrupted. "Where did you get that nickname?"

"Oh, that's another one of those long stories your 'friend' here was just talking about, so why don't we discuss it over dinner like I said. I'm even buying!"

Throughout dinner at the Charlton House, Raffe and Johnny exchanged stories about where they'd been and what they were doing, until the gunfighter mentioned his brief association with Cyrus Slaughter and Jennifer immediately commented on it angrily.

"My uncle was part of the plot to take Raffe's ranch away from him and get him sent to prison for five years, did you know that, Mr. Quick?"

"No, how could I? But remember, what I did for your uncle was strictly business. Nothing more, nothing less. It had nothing to do with the preacher here, even if I had known."

"I don't understand how you can separate the two like they have nothing to do with each other. Does it make your conscience rest easier by saying that?" Jennifer grew more irritated.

"I don't worry much about 'conscience,' Miss Mitchell. I'll leave that to you. My business has nothing to do with it."

"Jennifer." Raffe reached over, putting his hand on hers. "Let it go. It won't help anything to keep at it now."

"That's okay, preacher." Quick said, smiling easily. "I don't expect the lady to understand how I live or why. It even took you a little while to figure it out, didn't it? Now, why don't we just drop the subject and finish dinner. Then, I've got a poker game to attend to."

"We're going to get Raffe's ranch back one way or the other, and if it comes down to it, I hope by then you know who's side you're on." Jennifer got in one last jab.

"I'll bet you are, Miss Mitchell." Quick smiled that steely grin of his. "That's one fiery woman you got yourself, Raffe. You think you can handle her?"

Bart Hollister and his deputy pulled up in front of Slaughter's ranch, then went up the stairs into his private office. Slaughter exploded with the news of the savage gunfight.

"You hired this fast gun for those squatters, and now it turns out he helps Latimer right when those three hillbillies were about to finish him off—and with him all the trouble he's been causing around here since he came back!"

"How in this world was I to know that they knew each other? He never mentioned his name and neither did I, but that don't mean we still can't use him. Quick is a paid professional, and with him it's all business, if you know what I mean? His gun is for hire to the highest bidder. He don't care what it's for or who it's for so long as the money is right at the end of the job. I've got the notion that for enough cash he just might call out Latimer, so don't go get yourself all fired up until I find out if I'm right or not, and that ain't gonna take very long."

"You'd better do something soon, because the longer he's around, the more trouble comes from it. At the rate this thing is going I might have to call him out myself, even if I have to make up a charge."

"You just sit tight for a couple more days while I follow this thing through with Quick. There's plenty of time to take care of Latimer—I'll see to that!"

Early the next morning in the Double Eagle, Johnny was playing solitaire over at a corner table when Joe Cheek walked in, looking around the room. He spied Quick and walked over.

"Mr. Slaughter wants to see you back at the ranch, and he'd like you to ride back with me right now."

Quick continued turning cards without looking up, as the foreman fidgeted with his belt through several more seconds of silence. Finally, Johnny answered.

"You tell Mr. Slaughter that I haven't eaten breakfast yet, and I never discuss business until after I eat."

"He ain't gonna like being kept waiting, I'll tell you that right now."

"You ride back and tell the old man I'll be out later . . . maybe, if I can't get up a hand of poker. What's he want anyway, Cheek? You can save me a long ride."

"He didn't tell me that. Just said to come in and get you."

Quick shrugged, finally looking up. "You'd better get going and deliver my message."

"Okay. But he's gonna be awful unhappy about it."

Cheek stood there a moment longer, but when Johnny didn't respond, he finally turned and left.

After he'd eaten breakfast, Quick lit up a cigarillo and leaned back in the chair, wondering what the old man wanted now. Their business was over and done with, but he had mentioned that there might be something else just before Quick had left. Maybe he would ride out and see, just out of curiosity. One thing was for certain, Slaughter was a man of means, and he didn't mind spending when it suited him.

It was nearly noon when Johnny rode up to the ranch. He got down and tied off his horse. Cheek came out onto the porch to see who was there, then quickly went back inside. Quick was ushered into the office, where he saw Slaughter, sitting in his big easy chair behind the desk, glaring at him.

"You took your sweet time about gettin' out here! I thought you were a businessman?"

"That depends on the business, and who I'm doing it with. What do you want, Slaughter?"

The old man chewed on his cigar a moment longer, then stood up and came around the desk.

"You remember I told you I might just hire you out for another job, don'tcha?"

Johnny nodded slowly without answering.

"Well, now I've got it. I hear you helped this here convicted murderer named Latimer in town yesterday, is that right? You a friend of his, are you?"

"Yes, I helped him out, but it was by accident. Three men were about to shoot him in the back, and I just happened along in time to see it and dealt myself in. I don't like back shooters whoever they are. You want to take a man down you do it face-to-face. Why do you ask?"

"Because I either want him run out of town or shot dead, that's why. You name your price and I'll pay it, but I want it done without wasting any more time, you understand?"

Quick studied the old man's eyes for a moment as they stood close, for a man's eyes an tell more than his tongue. What he saw there was hatred, and even a flash of fear.

"I'll think on it," he answered. "And don't send Cheek to town looking for an answer. I'll let you know myself when I decide." Then he turned and started for the door.

"Well, don't take all week thinking about it. I want an answer, and I want it pretty quick, hear!"

The gunfighter just kept going until he was out the door.

Two days later, when Jennifer went back to her apartment after work, she found a note slid under the door. She quickly opened it.

"Jennifer—

I'll be gone four or five days down to the county seat at Loyalton looking for the federal circuit judge if he's there. If not I could stay a day or two longer on the chance he might show up. Be extra careful and take care of yourself until I get back.

R."

She folded the note carefully, then went across the room and put it into the top dresser drawer, wondering if Raffe would have any real chance at actually finding the traveling jurist. He was trying so hard—was so desperate for help—she wished there was more she could do, and felt the same frustration he did. At least no one in Loyalton would know or recognize him—he could walk the street without someone putting a gun on him or trying to lock him up—but still she was uneasy about the whole thing. He was so far away now, and it left her with a hollow feeling.

"Come back soon, Raffe," she whispered out loud to herself. "I need you here with me too."

She went into the kitchen and tried to prepare something to eat but her heart wasn't in it. She turned in early only to fall into a fitful sleep.

Chapter Seven

Old Acquaintances

When Raffe rode into Loyalton, he didn't have any trouble finding the county courthouse, a big two-story stone building down on one corner at the far end of town.

After stepping down, he looped his reins over the hitching post. He then dismounted with the strange feeling he was putting himself yet again into the hands of a system that had wrongly sent him to prison for five bitter years on false charges. For several moments he stood staring up at the gray stone structure, wondering if the law could make another mistake like the last one, and yet it seemed he had no other choice now if he wanted to clear his name and get Quiet Creek back. He took in a deep breath and started up the stairs.

The moment he stepped inside the heavy wooden double doors the cool, musty smell of books, paper, and polish assaulted his nostrils. He strode down the shiny wooden floors until he reached a door marked COUNTY CLERK, and stepped inside, where a little bespectacled man sat behind a desk, studying a thick sheaf of papers in an otherwise empty office. Raffe stopped at the counter and the man looked up without leaving his seat.

"Yes, can I help you?" he asked, peering through thick, owl-like glasses.

"Is this where the federal circuit judge holds court?"

"It is . . . when he's here."

"Well, is he here now?"

"No, he's not. He did come through here about five months ago, but he doesn't have a set schedule. And your name is?"

"Raffe Latimer. I'm down from Placer City. Is it always the same judge in here?" he questioned.

"Yes, that's Judge Barker, at least until they appoint someone else, but that isn't likely for a while yet. Do you have business with him?"

Raffe didn't want to go into details, and

made a vague reference to just wanting to talk to Barker about a personal legal matter.

"Well, you rode a long ways just to ask a few questions, so why don't you sit down at that desk over there and write them out. Then when he comes back through here I'll give them to him. You . . . can write, can't you?"

When Raffe was done he'd filled three full pages. He asked for an envelope.

"You'll be sure that Barker gets this, won't you? It's important to me—real important."

"I will, I'll put it on the desk in his chambers along with the other paperwork he'll have to go through, but like I said I don't know when that will be for sure. Now, is there anything else I can do for you?"

"Yes, there is. Do you know anyplace here in town where a man can stay without being gouged, and maybe get a square meal too?"

The little man thought for a moment, pen to his lips, then nodded.

"I'd say Mrs. Carrington's boardinghouse would probably fit that bill nicely. Her place is two blocks east of Main Street here. You can't miss it; she's got a big sign out front, it's a big two-story place. Her husband left it to her when he passed away several years ago and she had to fend for herself, but she's done real well by it. You might tell her that Fletcher Bird sent you over—that's me—she might even give you an extra dumpling in the stew."

When he walked up the stairs to Carrington's and knocked on the door, it took a few moments before a portly, middle-aged woman wearing an apron opened it. He introduced himself along with Bird's message.

"Oh yes—Mr. Bird. How nice of him to send you over. Please step in Mr. . . . Latimer. And will you be staying just today, or do you plan to stay over for a couple of days? You're just in time for lunch. Why don't you follow me into the dining room, and I'll introduce you to my other guests."

When they entered, seven other boarders, all men, were already eating. She seated him and gave everyone his name. He was greeted with only a casual glance and nod of hello in return, except for one man at the far end of the table who stopped, fork halfway to his mouth, and studied Latimer intently. As usual, Mrs. Carrington started up the conversation again, trying to entertain everyone and keep things lively.

"You here in Loyalton on business, Mr. Latimer?"

Raffe only nodded slightly and answered with a terse yes, starting to eat.

"Well, how nice . . . would you care to tell us what your business is?" she persisted.

"No, not really," he answered. Her smile faded, and she looked around the table for someone else more willing to be sociable, but got little help from the busily eating guests.

Later, after everyone had finished and left the table, only Raffe and the stranger at the end remained. The stranger got up to come over and sit next to Raffe, looking over his shoulder to be sure no one else was within earshot.

"You remember me?" His voice was barely above a whisper. Raffe turned to look him up and down then went back to his food.

"Nope, I don't."

"Well, I remember you all right, because I served you your meals through that little hole in the cell door when we was down in the territorial prison. Maybe you didn't get much of a look at me, the way they had you boys locked up in solitary living like vampires in the dark, but I seen a glimpse of you from time to time. Word had it that you shot down three bounty hunters, and all the boys upstairs were pullin' for you not to break. They even had bets on it!"

Raffe stopped eating and turned to study the bewhiskered man, his small, piglike eyes ablaze with envy.

"I lost track of you when they finally pulled you out, but you showed that darn Betterman he couldn't break you the way he did lots of other men. I seen 'em come outta there beggin' for mercy, down on their hands and knees, sayin' they'd do anything if he wouldn't stick 'em back in the hole. He used to enjoy it, the devil . . . By the way, my name's Coby Nite." He stuck out his hand. "It's a real pleasure meetin' you at last."

"Well, I'll tell you this." Raffe twisted in the chair and checked to be sure the room was still empty. "We'd both be a lot better off if you just keep all this to yourself. It's history now, and that's a good place for it to stay."

"Oh, you don't have to worry none about that. I know how the rest of these people on the outside act when they know you done hard time. I only made that mistake once when I tried to get a job and told 'em about being in prison. I got turned down cold everywhere I went, so I just kept my trap shut after that. Say, you live around here someplace?"

Latimer gave out as little information as possible, then asked Nite what he was doing in Loyalton. The little man leaned even closer to answer under his breath.

"Actually, I'm just passin' through here on

my way up to Placer City to meet two friends. We're goin' to do a little 'job,' if you know what I mean."

"What kind of job?"

"We hear there's a juicy little bank sittin' up there just wait in' to be relieved of all its cash. It's simple, quick, and easy. No bank guards, only a hick town sheriff, maybe one deputy. We're go in' there with scatterguns and clean out the place, then ride on out just like nothin' happened at all. There's a lot of cattle money up there."

"You in a hurry to get sent back down to prison?" Raffe challenged.

"I ain't never goin' back to prison, period. I swore to that the day I got out, and I meant it. I'll die before I let anyone try to take me back there!"

"It's just a matter of time before some law-man catches up to you, either in Placer City, or someplace else. Use your head. Find some-thing else to do."

"I already did and it didn't work. Now I'll do what I know best. Why heck, when I saw you come walk in' in here, the first thing I thought of was askin' you if you wanted in. We could use a man like you."

"No way. I got framed once, I'm not going give the law a reason to do it to me again. If

I was you I'd forget about it before you make a mistake you'll regret. There's no future in dodging the law for the rest of your life so you can wind up at the wrong end of a rope."

"I'll take my chances. What the heck, you only live once, don't you, so why not do it the way you want. I don't mind being on the wrong side of the law, because that's where I've been for most of my life anyway. But listen here. If you ain't comin' in with us, then just forget we ever had this little talk, because we're still gonna take down that bank."

Raffe pushed back from the table and got to his feet, shooting a quick glance at Nite for a moment, purposely keeping Jennifer Mitchell's name out of it.

"If you three go in there it's a fool's play, but it's your neck. Just remember I told you so." He turned and walked out the door.

Late that night, after everyone had turned in, Raffe sat on the bed in his room thinking about the planned robbery. There was a small knock on the door, and he got up to open it just slightly, surprised to find Martha Carrington.

"I hope I haven't bothered you, Mr. Latimer, but I saw your light under the door and just wanted to be sure you didn't need anything before I turned in too."

"Well, no, there's nothing I need," Raffe replied.

"Do you mind if I step in for just a moment? I feel a little odd standing out here in the hall of my own house."

He hesitated a moment longer, noticing that she'd shed her apron, taken her dark brown hair down so it now fell to her shoulders, and even changed dresses.

"I always check on my guests before turning in . . . Do you have enough blankets . . . fresh wash water in the basin?" She stepped closer, until finally he relented and she came inside. Raffe retreated back to the bed, pulling up a pair of saddlebags and sorting through them as she took a slow turn, checking out the room. Raffe wondered what she was really doing there.

"You know, this room used to be one of our guest rooms—that is, my late husband and I— before he passed away. I used to work for him taking care of the place and when he became a widower I guess he thought I already knew the place from top to bottom, so why not ask me to marry him? It was what they call a June-December sort of marriage. He was a lot older than me but gentle, not demanding. It was a sort of business partnership, I guess you could say, not like two young people madly in love.

We entertained his friends and business acquaintances mostly, but I guess some of that business must have rubbed off on me, because when he died I took over the place on my own, and I've been running it ever since. I guess you could say I'm about the only businesswoman in this whole town. A lot of people resent it, especially other women, but they all have husbands to take care of them. Do you know what I mean?"

"Yes, Mrs. Carrington, I believe I do." He still wondered why she was telling him all this.

"Please just call me Martha. Mrs. Carrington is all right down at the dinner table, but not up here ... after hours. Now, what's a good-looking man like you doing traveling alone? Do you have a wife and house full of kids waiting for you back where you came from, or are you one of those men that likes to be footloose and fancy-free?"

She stopped puttering around and took several steps toward him with a strange look in her eyes, her hands on her hips as she stared him straight in the face.

"No, I don't have any children, at least not yet, but I do have someone, a woman who means a lot to me, and that's all I'll say about it. I'm not looking for anything else. I hope you understand. I don't want to hurt your feelings or anyone else's for that matter. I'm here on business, and that's the only reason I'm here. I hope we understand each other?"

The breakfast table was busy as boarders dug into the grub and made small talk. Raffe glanced to the end of the table where Martha Carrington sat prim and proper carrying on a conversation with one of the guests. She shot a knowing glance quickly his way. He studied her for a moment longer, wondering what made some woman tick, then he poured himself a cup of strong black coffee, trying to forget their strange little encounter.

Later that morning he went back to the courthouse. He was met by the surprised look of the clerk.

"You were just here yesterday. Nothing's changed. Judge Barker still isn't here, and probably won't be for a good while."

"I just thought I'd try while I'm still here. I'm only going to be around another day or so. If I could just talk to him face-to-face it would be so much easier to explain what I want to tell him."

"I understand that, but like I said, it could be weeks or months before he returns, and nobody—including me—knows for sure when that might be. Are you staying at Mrs. Carrington's?"

Raffe nodded.

"Well then, if he actually did come in I'd get word to you, all right?"

After Raffe left he did a slow walk around town, noting it was larger and busier than Placer City, with horsemen and creaking wagons riding up and down the street, some loaded with women and children. Even though he was a stranger here, it was a relief not to be known or noticed as he moved along the wooden sidewalks. Back up north he always had to watch his back, either from Hollister, or someone else he didn't even know who had a grudge against him like the McCannlises.

Later, he passed by a saloon on the opposite side of the street. Looking in briefly, he spotted Nite standing at the bar. Nite saw him, and called out. "Latimer, c'mon in here and have a whiskey with me. I'm buying!"

Raffe paused, glancing around the interior, as Nite urged him in again. "One little drink isn't going to hurt you none."

He finally stepped inside and made his way over to the bar where Nite had already called up another glass. The squirrelly man then steered Raffe over to a table with a fresh bottle.

"Well, you been thinkin' about what I said?" he asked, a sly smile parting his salt-and-pepper beard.

"No, I haven't. Like I told you before, you'd better forget the whole thing. You're only asking for trouble if you keep at it."

Nite's eyes narrowed as he took another slurp of whiskey, studying the big man across the table. Then he continued.

"What in tarnation happened to you down there in prison anyway? Did they boil all the grit out of you, or what?"

"No, I just got a lot smarter, and you'd better learn some of it too. You think it's worth spending the rest of your life on the run because of some two-bit bank job, or wondering if the next time you turn around there's a bellyful of buckshot waiting for you? There's no bank in Colorado or anyplace else worth that and especially not in Placer City. Besides, I got a friend who works there, and I won't see her harmed in any way."

"A friend—you mean a woman friend? Why heck, we ain't goin' in there to harm no one. You just tell her to stay out of the way and we'll be in and out in no time flat."

"That's a chance I'm not going to take. If you and these partners of yours can't get it through your head that Placer City isn't worth it, then you'd better tell them to head for some-place else. There's nothing in that bank worth taking in the first place except a lot of trouble, and you'll probably have the sheriff and half the town down your back before you can reach your horses. You'd better think double hard on what I'm telling you while you've still got the chance. Don't do it. It won't work."

Raffe got to his feet, finishing the drink, then walked out the door, leaving Nite sitting there shaking his head in disgust.

Raffe made one more visit to the courthouse the next afternoon, still without success, then prepared to leave the following morning. Just before dinner was served he informed Martha Carrington that he'd settle his bill after eating so he could get an early start.

"Oh, I'll be up before you go tomorrow. That's part of keeping this place going. You can pay me then. It's too bad you're leaving so soon. You've hardly had time to really see the town and the country around it."

She stood in the kitchen working over the big woodstove, then paused for a moment to turn and look past him into the dining room. The other boarders were already busy in con-versation with each other, waiting for dinner to be served.

"I hope . . . you don't think too badly of me, you know, for the other night?" Her face flushed slightly.

"I don't." He tried to rectify the tense, uncomfortable situation. "You're an attractive woman that I'm sure any man around here would be proud to have on his arm. There's probably a whole tableful right in there." He jerked a thumb over his shoulder at the table, but she just shook her head.

"No, not in there, Mr. Latimer." She kept her voice low. "They're just customers, not real company, not what a woman really wants. Now, you'd better get to the table. I'm about to serve it up."

Early the next morning, Raffe went downstairs to find her already in the kitchen, even though the dining room was still empty.

"Well, good morning." She smiled at him. "Are you going to eat breakfast before you leave us? No sense in starting that long ride back to Placer City on an empty stomach, is there?"

"No, I guess not, not if you feel like cooking something up this early."

"Of course I will. Why don't you go in there and make yourself comfortable, and I'll bring in a fresh pot of hot coffee."

After eating alone he headed for the parlor room office to find her busy going over the bills.

"All ready to go?" She looked up.

"I guess I am. Let's settle up on what I owe you."

"You don't owe me a thing, Mr. Latimer, not a red cent. You're paid up in full. Meals go with the board. I don't charge extra for them. Can I tell you something else before you go?" She arched an eyebrow, but before Raffe could answer, she went on.

"Your woman, whoever she is, is one lucky lady to have a man like you. I hope she knows that and appreciates what she's got. You ever come back this way, please be sure to stop in and at least say hello, will you?"

Raffe nodded, smiling slightly, then thanked her and headed for the door. Just as he lifted the saddlebags up on his horse, the door swung open and Coby Nite came running down the stairs.

"You're pullin' out, huh? Well, just remember our little talk. We'll be up your way pretty quick, maybe even sometime this week, so when you see me in town, just tell this friend of yours to take a couple of days off like I said before. That way no one gets hurt."

"You'd better remember what I told you.

You and your friends are asking for more trouble than you can handle, and if I have to get mixed up in it I will. Forget about it while you've still got the chance, Coby, because you won't get another one."

"Unnh-unnh. Not likely. My friends have ridden too far to just walk away now. I don't want to tangle with you, Raffe, you know that, but even you can't take down three men without catching a bullet yourself. If you don't want in, then stay out of it, because we mean to do our 'business' up there one way or the other."

The big man pulled himself up in the saddle and looked down at Nite with a cold stare that spoke volumes. He then pulled the horse around and started down the street, leaving the little man muttering under his breath, until he finally started back up the stairs into the boardinghouse.

Chapter Eight

Best Laid Plans

Bronc Hook looked across the campfire flames at his brother Boge, who was slowly stirring a can of simmering beans.

"So, what do you figure, another day or maybe two to Placer City?"

Boge didn't look up, but nodded with a grunt, turning his head slightly to spit a brown stream of tobacco juice into the night wind.

"You be sure and keep that outta them beans." Bronc scowled. "They already got enough grit in 'em as it is. Now, listen here. When we meet up with Nite, I want to spend a day or two just timing the bank and lookin' around town some. After that we can go in and take it, and whatever else looks good all at the same time, like a dry goods store close by, and kill two birds with one stone. Then in all the confusion we'll slip outta a town just like we did down in Kellsyville last year, remember?"

"Of course I remember." Boge rocked back on his haunches, leaving the stick in the can, and studying his brother for a moment through a bushy black beard. "I ain't worried none about you and me, it's that Nite I don't trust. He talks too much. No tellin' who he's shot his mouth off to. It woulda been better if just you and me did the job and got out like we usually do. I know you'll cover my back and me yours, but are you sure he would if things got tight? I've never been on a job with him before, have you? Remember, that's our neck stickin' out too, know what I mean?"

"Yeah, I do, but he's the one who put us on to Placer City in the first place." Bronc replied. "Besides, we'll be sure he knows what he's doing before we make our move. He was in on that stage job a couple of months back over at Twin Buttes, so he's got to know something. Now, let's eat them beans and turn in. We still got a pretty good ride ahead of us before we get to town. Then we can have some real food. This boiled-over coffee is getting a little stale, just like them hard rock beans."

The Hook brothers reached Placer City two days later. They rode casually down Main Street, eyeing the businesses and buildings lining the boardwalk, looking carefully at the bank, where Boge grunted, nodding quickly at the structure. A little farther along, Bronc called out to a man crossing the street in front of them.

"Hey mister, you got a ho-tel in this here town?"

The stranger directed them to the Double Eagle, where a few minutes later they dismounted and unbuckled their saddlebags. As they pulled their rifles out and started up the stairs to go inside, a young boy walked past.

"Say kid. You wanna earn two bits?" Bronc said, stopping him. "Take these two horses down to whatever you got for a livery stable and have 'em unsaddled, then get them a good feed, you hear?"

"Sure will, sir. Mr. Daniel's got a six-horse stable, and even a boy to clean it up. I'll take 'em over there."

"Well, go do it then." Hook tossed him the coins, then turned for the door.

Inside, several men were sitting reading the local newspaper and most glanced up briefly as they walked by, studying the trail-worn pair, noting their long, dirty dusters, saddlebags over their shoulders, and especially their packing rifles.

"We want a room," Bronc said, as he laid his gear on the counter, eyeing the clerk. "How much for both of us, one bed?"

"It's four dollars a night if you don't want dirty clothes picked up and washed, and four-fifty if you do. And if you don't mind me asking, do you really think it's necessary to pack all that iron in here? This is a hotel, not a shooting gallery."

Both men stared hard at the clerk without answering before Bronc tossed the money across the counter.

"Well, why don't you just mind your own business and keep your lip buttoned while you're at it. The only other thing we wanna know outta you is whether anyone named Nite checked in here already."

"Nite? No, no one by that name."

"Then give me the key to our room so we can go up and see what's worth four dollars a night. If he does come in you tell him the Hook brothers are upstairs, and save the smart mouth for someone else."

Later that night the brothers walked around town, stopping in front of the bank. They tried to peek around the closed steel shutters over the front windows, but couldn't see inside. As they stooped lower, a voice right behind them brought them both up short.

"What do you boys think you're doing?" Clint Richie stepped up off the dirt street and confronted them.

"Doin' . . . we weren't doin' nothing. Who the hell are you, anyway?" Bronc was indignant.

"I'm the deputy sheriff around here, that's who. Now how about answering a few questions, like what do you think you're doing?"

"Well . . . we're new in town, and was just out for a walk lookin' things over, that's all. There ain't no law against that is there?" Bronc shot back.

"See what it says on the door, Placer City Bank? How much more do you need to know than that? You can read, can't you? What's your names anyway?"

"Names? . . . Ah, I'm Smith, Jim Smith, and this here's my brother, Bill." Bronc tried hard to sound convincing.

"Smith, huh? Maybe I'll just look that up back in the sheriff's office. Now why don't you two just move along. By the way, are you staying in town . . . Bill?" Richie leveled a gaze at Bronc, knowing he was lying through his teeth.

"Yeah, we are, over at the hotel. Just got in tonight, but we're only gonna stay for a day or two then head out. There ain't much else to keep us here."

"All right, now find someplace else to hang out for the night," Richie ordered, and with that the brothers turned and started back up the street to the Double Eagle, talking under their breaths once they were out of earshot.

Back inside the Double Eagle, the bar was alive with customers, and the pair bellied up to the bar. Bronc ordered a whiskey, then glanced slowly around the crowded room at the men busy gambling at the faro tables and in the poker room further back, where a group of by-standers stood around the table watching the action. A few moments later they took their drinks and pushed back there too, eyeing the players as they came up. They looked espe-cially hard at one man, who was neatly dressed in a black suit and string tie. He seemed to be winning big, the chips stacked in neat rows in front of him. He lit another thin cigar and glanced up at the newcomers for an instant while the shuffle was in progress.

In that one glance, Johnny Quick learned all he needed to about the dirty, whiskered pair. This skill was something he always prided himself on—reading people instantly, their lifestyle, intelligence, often even their line of work. That kind of natural ability went hand in hand with his profession, and was imperative to his success in gunplay, when it came to that. He knew the unkempt pair weren't town dwellers, that they lived on the edge of society even in that unruly time, and had probably had their share of run-ins with the law—had maybe even served jail time. He'd seen dozens of other men like them and wouldn't forget their ugly, thick whiskered faces. Then it was time to get back to the cards, and the three eights he'd just been dealt.

"That there's Johnny Quick." One of the onlookers leaned over to Bronc, whispering under his breath. "He's giving the houseman a real run for his money, ain't he?"

"Looks like a card hawk to me." Bronc's voice was loud enough that several men turned to look at him. "Anyone dumb enough to waste their money on them cardboards deserves to lose his money!"

He took another sip at the whiskey, glaring back at the circle of men and not caring if they liked what he'd said or the way he'd said it.

"Keep your voice down, mister." The dealer turned in his chair. "If you want to make noise, go back at the bar, not in here. We've got a serious card game going on, or can't you see that?"

Boge tugged at his brother's sleeve, jerking him back toward the main room.

"Idiots!" the dealer snapped. "Never seen a bar of soap or spring bed in their whole lives, then come in here shooting off their dirty mouths. How many cards, Quick?"

Later that same night Raffe quietly rode back into town and went directly to Jennifer's apartment, knocking lightly on the door until she got up out of bed sleepily asking who it was. When she finally opened up she threw both arms around his neck and held him tightly, whispering how glad she was to see him back.

"Guess what?" She touched his head with both hands, a smile breaking out across her face. Then she kissed him quickly.

"I've got the papers from the bank right here. I put them in the bottom drawer of my dresser!"

She broke away to retrieve them. Raffe made his way to the kitchen table, then sat down to study the documents carefully, reading them under the glow of the kerosene lamp. He looked up when he was done.

"This is it, this is what I've needed all along if I'm ever going to get Quiet Creek back. I hope no one finds out they're gone before I get the chance to show them to the right people. You've done more good with this than you can almost imagine." He reached up, wrapping his arm around her waist and pulling her close. "I don't know what I'd do without you." She caressed his long hair, happy to hear him say that.

"Were you able to see the circuit judge down in Loyalton?" She'd almost forgotten about the trip, lost in the moment, as he explained the disappointing results.

"Don't worry about it, Raffe. Things are finally starting to go our way. It will work itself out, I can almost feel it now. I missed you so much, even though it was only a few days. When you're gone I feel so . . . incomplete it scares me. I've never felt that way before, never really needed anyone that much. I guess I really realized for the first time how much I love you and depend on you to make things right. Now that you're back I can breathe again."

She pulled his head close against her, still standing, and began working her fingers deep into his shoulders. He let his head drop, soaking up the massage.

"Don't try to ride all the way back to camp tonight. Stay here on the couch. I'll get some blankets for you. Okay?"

Raffe lay awake long after Jennifer went back into the bedroom and fell asleep. She trusted him so completely it was astounding, and that was a trust he would not break. Finally, he pulled the blanket up under his chin and dozed off.

The next morning, Coby Nite rode down the deserted streets of Placer City and found the hotel. He went in and asked if the Hooks were registered there. In a few minutes, he was pounding on their door. Buck finally answered, still half asleep.

Meanwhile, Raffe and Jenny were sipping hot coffee as he told her about the plans to hold up the bank. He then asked her not to go to work until he found out if the three men were actually in town.

"I can't do that Raffe. I can't just stay away—I've got to go to work, or it would only draw attention to me. Maybe those men gave up on the idea after you talked to this Nite. You know, it might have just been whiskey talk and nothing more."

"No." Raffe shook his head slowly. "It wasn't that. They're not going to forget it.

They'll show up here sooner or later, and when they do, I'll have to try and stop them. I don't want to show myself around town any more than I have to, but I'll have to get out and see what I can find, avoiding Hollister and that deputy of his. He's just itching to find an excuse to try and jail me, but I'm not going to let that happen, not now or any other time. I'll just have to be careful about it."

As Nite and the brothers talked about the bank job, Nite also told them about his meeting with Latimer in Loyalton, and his threat not to let them go through with it.

"Sounds like he might be trouble." Buck scratched at his beard. "Maybe we'll just have to take care of him too while we're at it."

"Well, I reckon he could be trouble," Nite agreed. "He ain't one to make threats and forget about 'em; that's why I'm bringin' it up right now before we do anything more. We're gonna have to keep an eye out for him."

"I ain't lettin' no jailbird mess up this job, not after Boge and I had to ride so far to get here. If he gets in the way, I'll cut him in half with a shotgun," Buck threatened.

"I already tried to tell him to just stay out of it, but it didn't work. We can't miss him. He's a big man—about six-one—with long brown hair nearly down to his shoulders and light green eyes. He nearly always wears a tan hat and buckskin shirt, along with a gun belt studded with them silver conchos. If we're going to spend a couple of days looking things over, there's a good chance we'll run into him. Then we can figure out how to take him."

Later that afternoon Nite sat across the street from the bank on a bench outside the feed store casually having a smoke while he watched the Hooks go into the building on the pretense of opening an account. Inside, the brothers took in the cages, the number of employees, the big walk-in vault in back, and Everheardt sitting at his desk studying a sheaf of papers. Then Boge leaned over and whispered in his brother's ear, "Lookit that cashier over there . . . now that's one whole lot of woman, ain't it?"

But Buck only shook his head, meaning that Boge should shut up, then both men turned and started for the door. As Jenny finished with her customer she called out, "I'll be right with you if you can wait a moment?"

"Naw, that's all right." Buck waved a hand. "We'll be back later."

Across the street, Nite watched them come out, then all three headed back to the hotel. Even the quick look Jenny had gotten of the scruffy strangers brought back Raffe's warning about a possible robbery, and that afternoon when she finished work and headed back to her apartment, she told Raffe about the men, even though the description didn't fit Coby Nite. Raffe didn't say much as he thought it over, then finally looked up at her.

"I've got an idea that just might work . . . maybe."

The next morning, when Richie unlocked the sheriff's office, he found a folded note slipped under the door and picked it up to read.

"There are three men in town who mean to rob the bank, probably sometime in the next two or three days. Be warned."

"The darn thing isn't even signed," Hollister grumbled to Richie. "Any crackpot could have wrote something like this."

"I don't know, Bart. There's something about it that sorta rings true to me, you know what I mean? Why would anyone write something like that as a joke, it doesn't make any sense. Besides, I've seen some characters around here lately that fit the bill pretty darn good. What could it hurt if we figured it's true no matter who wrote it or why? Don't you think we'd be smart if we looked out for it to happen and maybe stopped it before it was too late?"

Hollister poured a cup of coffee, then sat down at his desk and thought things over as he sipped at the cup.

"Well, maybe. I'll have a talk with Eaverhardt and see what we can come up with."

That afternoon when the bank closed, Hollister sat across from Everheardt and explained his concerns about a possible hold-up, suggesting a plan he'd been concocting.

"Well, I guess we could try something like that if you really feel it's necessary." Everheardt replied. You know, we've never had a robbery, even an attempted one, all these years. Are you that sure someone is going to try something like that?"

"No, I'm not, but I can't take the chance either. I think we ought to try it for at least a day or two, and if nothing happens, then I'll call it a hoax. But, if someone does try to pull it off, then Clint and I will be right there in the building to stop them."

The little man nodded slowly, then looked the sheriff in the eye with a greedy gleam.

"By the way, how's our little 'business' going out at Clear Creek? I've purposely stayed away from there and Cyrus's too lately, but I've naturally been thinking about it."

"It's doing just fine. We took out about six thousand dollars in gold last month. Slaughter keeps track of it at his place until he's got about ten grand or so, then takes Cheek and a couple of men and rides down to Loyalton to cash it in. He doesn't want to draw any attention to himself around here, so it's worth the long ride for that kind of money. Then when he deposits it here everything is on the up-and-up. Haven't you checked your account lately?"

"No, I've been too busy with other matters, but I meant to shortly, and I don't keep that close a track on the mining end like you do."

"Well, it's going all right, and now if I could just put Latimer behind bars for good it would go even better. You haven't seen him around town lately, have you?"

Evarhardt shook his head, but in the same moment, Jennifer Mitchell came to mind.

"Didn't you tell me that Jennifer Mitchell actually bailed him out of jail a couple of weeks back? She works here for me, you know."

"Yeah, I knew that. I don't know what in the world her connection is with the likes of him, but she did post his bail, even though it cost her her place out at Slaughter's. He threw her out, clothes and all. I think she's got a place here in town, but I haven't taken the time to find out where. Maybe I will once this bank thing is settled one way or the other."

The next morning before the bank opened, both Hollister and Richie donned clerk's shirts as the manager tried to familiarize them with their daily business—the cages—and then explained their presence to the other employees, assuring them nothing would happen if they just followed orders. Jennifer was especially uncomfortable with their presence, but tried to hide it with her businesslike manner, avoiding any personal conversation with either man. Just before the doors opened the lawmen slid two six-guns under the counter near the cages, then warned everyone that should a robbery attempt actually take place they were to comply and hand over the cash until the robbers turned to leave, then hit the floor when he and Richie made their move. Then Eaverhardt went to the front door and opened the bank for business.

That first day was long, boring, and uneventful as both men tried to busy themselves with tasks unfamiliar, while also studying each and every person who entered the bank. They already knew most who came in, and several came over to ask what they were doing there. Hollister hushed them without an answer. When they closed that afternoon, Jennifer rushed home to tell Raffe about the two men, but she found he was already gone. He had left a short note asking her to stay home again, but not explaining where he'd gone, why, or when he'd return. Unpleasant as it was, she was still determined to go to work the next day and not draw attention to herself by being absent.

Raffe rode steadily away from town, after unsuccessfully looking for Coby Nite, arriving at his hidden hunting camp that afternoon. After restocking it with the few supplies he'd brought in, he saddled back up and rode along the timber ridges that led back to Quiet Creek and the mining going on there. He quietly dismounted, moving carefully down through thick woods, until he could just make out the tiny figures of men far below through the trees. He could see that several new guards had been added around the sluice boxes and on both sides of the creek. His earlier surveillance had clearly prompted their presence. Satisfied the mining was still going on full tilt, he slipped away back uphill and headed for camp. Later, by a small fire in front of the dugout, he thought about all that had happened since he was sent to prison, and what might happen in the days and weeks ahead as he tried to get his ranch back and at the same time prove that some of the most powerful and influential men in the country were the ones who had taken it from him illegally. It was overwhelming.

The next morning at ten o'clock sharp the bank opened for business, and once again the sheriff and his deputy were on hand, pretending to busy themselves with paperwork as the first customers came in. It was just an hour later when Coby Nite rode up in front of the building. He tied off his horse, then got down and walked around to the alley in back, retrieving two more mounts and leading them back around front next to his.

Shortly, the Hooks appeared, coming down the boardwalk wearing their long, dirty dusters. They passed Nite with a quick nod, then checked up and down the street momentarily before entering the bank. Inside, Buck quickly noticed only two people at the window, a woman and her young daughter. Boge stood back against the door to block anyone else from coming in. Neither man noticed the two new workers busying themselves with paperwork, but the two lawmen quickly flashed knowing glances at each other, then at the six-guns hidden under the counter only a few feet away.

The woman was at Jenny's window when Buck walked up and unceremoniously pulled her away, ordering everyone not to make a move while waving his pistol around the suddenly silent room.

"This is a stickup, and if you stand right still and do what you're told, you won't get yourself shot full of holes. Understood?"

He pointed the .45 directly at Jennifer's face with a grim glare.

"You . . . clean out those money drawers and be quick about it. Hurry up! Boge, if anyone tries anything, let 'em have it."

At his desk, Everheardt froze in terror, trying to sink down lower and make himself even smaller than he was. Hollister took one very slow step toward the counter as Buck's attention was riveted on gathering the money. Buck caught his move out of the corner of his eye.

"You take one more step like that and I'll drop you where you stand. Boge, get over here and keep an eye on this one. You, missy, hurry up with that cash, and clean out the drawers on each side too."

Jennifer quickly scooped the cash into the large sack until it was nearly full, then stepped back to her cage, pushing it across to the gunman.

"You done real good." Buck forced a twisted smile, as the young girl standing with her mother broke down and began crying hysterically. The petrified woman pulled her to her breast trying to quiet her, and the brothers' attention was momentarily distracted as they looked at the pair.

In that instant, both Hollister and Richie dove for their weapons, yelling for everyone to hit the floor. They came up shooting through the cage bars at the startled pair, and Boge screamed out, then sagged to the floor, shot through the stomach. He pulled himself around and tried to crawl for the door. Buck spun around firing at the sheriff as fast as he could pull the trigger, then swung over toward the deputy, hitting Richie before Hollister hit him with a bullet straight through the forehead. He fell like a sack of potatoes, quivering in instant death, eyes bulging from the impact of hot lead.

Outside, Nite heard the sudden explosion of gunfire and saw blurred figures flashing behind the windows. Instantly knowing something had gone wrong, he hesitated between jumping off his horse and running to help, or pulling the horse around and riding away as fast as he could go. Before he could make his decision, the sheriff burst through the door and ordered him off the horse. Nite drew his pistol and fired, driving the lawman back inside. He then yanked the reins around and thundered down the street on a streaking run to get away.

He pounded past storefronts and buildings

and made it halfway down the street and almost around the first corner to safety, when a
tall shadowed figure stepped from an alley leveling a rifle at him. As the fleeing man sped
past, a single shot sent him tumbling backwards off the saddle. He hit the ground with a
squashy thud and rolled to a dead stop, a fatal
bullet burning deep in his chest. He gasped for
breath, then relaxed in death.

Townspeople and businessmen spilled from
the buildings yelling and pointing up and down
the street. Hollister exited the bank and looked
up the dirt wheel track to see Nite piled in a
heap. No one seemed to know who had fired
the deadly shot. Much later, after the dead had
been taken away by Johnson Sloan, the under-
taker, and Richie's arm wound had been sewn
up, the sheriff sat in his office, trying to un-
ravel the sudden and troubling turn of events.
Who had written that note, and how could that
person know what was going to happen, yet
not be involved in some way? Who had killed
the third robber as he fled down Main Street,
then simply disappeared without taking credit
for stopping him? The whole affair gave Hollister an eerie feeling that this and other recent
events were beginning to spin out of his control. That was a feeling that ate at him just as
much as the mystery itself, for he was not a

man to let his power and authority be either questioned or taken away. The more he went over and over the events in his mind, the more he was convinced it was time to call for a meeting of his partners Slaughter, Everheardt, Richie, and himself, and the sooner the better.

Chapter Nine

The Manhunt

Two days after the murderous shoot-out at the bank, when things had begun to die down somewhat, Hollister carried out his intention to bring the four men together for a discussion about his concerns. They met at Slaughter's ranch that Wednesday night after dark, gathering in Cyrus's office. He gave strict orders to Martha not to be disturbed for any reason, then pulled the doors shut and nodded for everyone to sit down as he lit one of his strong Mexican cigars.

"I've brought my foreman in on this because he'll likely be needed, from what Bart's told me so far. Now what's the rest of this all about?" Slaughter turned to the sheriff, twisting in his big, leather-padded easy chair.

Hollister went over the killings, especially the third man killed by someone still unknown, the prophetic note that outlined the hold up attempt, the word that someone had been seen out at the old Quiet Creek ranch, and Cyrus's own concerns about the man who'd been run off while spying on the gold-washing operation on the creek. He paused, then turned to Slaughter, taking a long sip on his whiskey glass and letting the words sink in before finishing.

"I've thought about this a lot, and come to the conclusion that there's only one thing that's changed around here in the last five years that might have something to do with it. That something is the return of Raffe Latimer. He could be the lynchpin to this whole deal. I can't think of anyone else, can you?" He looked around at the others, but there was no answer.

"I didn't think so. Now, I say we find out just where he's been holing up, and do something about him once and for all."

"Like what?" Slaughter leaned back, slowly blowing a cloud of smoke toward the ceiling.

"Like getting rid of him once and for all, that's what." Hollister replied. "We should have done it the day he rode back into town and showed his face, and I darn near had him until your niece showed up and bailed him out of jail."

Slaughter pursed his lips, trying to control his sudden anger at the mention of her name, and took in a deep breath before answering.

"That's why she's no longer here. But I don't think we have to worry about her over this."

"I'm not so sure, Mr. Slaughter," Richie put in. "Maybe she's been seeing Latimer and trying to help him out in some other way. After all, she was mighty quick in getting him out on bail, wasn't she, Bart?"

"She was, but I don't know exactly where she's staying." Hollister turned to his deputy. "Do you?"

"No, but it wouldn't be too hard to find out if we want to."

"Ah . . . gentlemen, I know where Miss Mitchell is living." Everyone turned to stare at Everheardt as he twisted uncomfortably in his chair.

"You know, how in the world do you know that?" Slaughter rested both arms on the chair and stared hard at the little man.

"I just had some . . . business to discuss with her after hours, so I looked up her address in personal records, that's all. It was just a short

visit, she didn't even . . . let me in actually."
His voice trailed off.

"All right then, that's a start. Where's she
staying?" Hollister questioned.

"One block over from Main Street, behind
Hemsteads' storage barn. It's a little apartment
on the ground floor, just as you turn into the
alley. I believe Hemstead's wife rents it out, if
I'm not mistaken."

"All right then, that's a start. He could be
holing up there, or maybe he just comes into
town visiting it from time to time. We'll start
keeping an eye on the place."

The banker, still looking uncomfortable, put
his soft white hand atop the desk for support,
cleared his throat slightly, and continued.

"If you don't mind me asking, even if you
do find him, what do you intend to do about
it? I mean, he hasn't broken any laws he could
be jailed for, has he?"

"He'll just disappear!" Cyrus was quick with
the answer.

"Disappear? You don't mean . . . like murder, do you? I have to tell you right now that
I won't be a part to anything like that. Ac-
quiring Quiet Creek Ranch was one thing, but
now you're talking about something we could
all hang for. You can count me out if that's
what you've got in mind."

"Hold on a minute, all of you. None of us will have to get involved if you'll just shut up and listen to me." Cyrus waved a finger.

"I've got just the man to take care of Latimer, just like he took care of Altman and them squatters of his out at Big Meadow. I can have Joe, here, fetch him out to the ranch for a little talk, and that talk is all about money. That's what he understands. Now you let me get ahold of him, then we'll see what happens before anyone else gets all upset. Latimer has got to go and I don't care how. Neither should any of you. From what I've heard here he may already know way too much for his own good, so you just let me talk to this Quick before anyone goes flying off the handle saying what they will and won't do. Quick can solve all this with one pull of the trigger while we stay in the clear if there's any trouble over it.

"Bart, you and Richie keep your eyes open back in town, while I have Joe and some of the men start looking up in the hills in case he's holed up there someplace. Everheardt, you keep an eye on my niece, and see what you can find out from her without being too obvious. She works for you and is there every day. See what you can learn. Now that we've got our heads together, let's go to work and get some results. I don't believe it'll be too long before Mr. Latimer is no longer with us, and I say the sooner the better!"

The next morning, Slaughter sent Cheek and several men out scouring the hills above the gold diggings where they had seen and shot at the shadowy intruder, while the old man himself rode into town looking for Johnny Quick. He found him at the Double Eagle eating breakfast. Quick was slightly surprised to see him there but invited him to sit down while he ate. Slaughter immediately made his proposition, leaning forward to keep his voice low, as Johnny forked up another mouthful of eggs.

"Take out Latimer, huh? What are you willing to pay for a job like that?" He asked matter-of-factly.

"I'll give you three thousand cash money, but I want it done quick, no messing around. I want him dead right now, not next week or next month."

"What's your rush?"

"That's my business. Yours is to find him and get rid of him soon as possible. Then you can pick up your money and clear out before anyone has the chance to ask any questions. Well, what's it gonna be, you want the job or not?"

"Let me think on it, then I'll get back to you."

"I told you I ain't got time for that. I want an answer now or I'll find someone else."

"Someone else? You're a little too old to be kidding yourself, aren't you? There's no one else around here who's going to go up against Latimer, and both you and I know it. He's not some dumb cowhand you can run off with a scare. He's killed men, you know that, and he knows how to handle a six-gun. I'll either do it my way or I won't do it at all. Then I'll decide whether or not I can take him out, period. He could be fast, maybe not as fast as me, but fast. I want an edge when things are cut that thin, and that's my deal—take it or leave it."

"You'd just better be quick about it, like I said. I'm not gonna wait around for you, gunslinger or not. I can't afford the time anymore for an long set-up." Slaughter stared back hard at the dapper killer.

"If you don't mind, I'd like to finish eating my breakfast without arguing with you. You know what I'm willing to do, but it's going to be my way, period."

Slaughter got to his feet and stormed out of the room, knowing Quick was right and he had little choice. All he could hope for now was that Quick would find Latimer fast and do what he said. Then he headed for the sheriff's office to find Hollister.

"I've got Richie keeping an eye on your niece's place just in case he shows up there, and I told him if he did, not to call him out on his own but to come and get me first. Two of us have a better chance of taking him down if he does try to pull on us. Did you find Quick?"

Slaughter related his heated conversation. For several moments more Hollister did not answer as he thought it over.

"That's all right. The more people we have out looking for him the better, even if Quick doesn't move right away. He'll go for the deal because he's a money-grubber and he can't resist it. You watch. Now, what about Joe, you got him out too?"

The foreman and his men worked their way slowly uphill through dog-hair timber until topping out. Cheek then had an Indian named Sam Cocker get down and look for tracks. The quiet man knelt down, his keen black eyes studying the slight impression in thick pine needles. In a moment, he looked up.

"One man rode this way maybe . . . two days ago."

"Can you follow it?" Cheek asked.

"Maybe so."

"Then let's get going. You get in the lead. C'mon boys!"

Two hours later, they dismounted, moving down quietly through the trees, guns drawn. They closed in on Raffe's hidden camp, only to find it empty.

"He's sure as heck been holing up here, all right. Lookit all this food." Cheek swung his gun barrel around. "Sam, you and three of the boys stay right here in case Latimer comes back, and if he does, don't ask any questions. Drop him soon as you can. I'm going to take the rest of the men and head back to the ranch to tell Slaughter what we've found. You stay here tonight and no fires, understand? If he don't show by sunup, then you come back in. Remember to use your rifles, and don't miss. Now, we're gonna kick. I'll see you back there one way or the other, and I hope you bring in good news when you come."

Later that day a buckboard came rattling down Main Street in Placer City. It was commandeered by a gray-bearded man sitting bolt upright, wearing a dusty black suit and top hat, a bulging briefcase and suitcase tied just behind the seat. He pulled the horse to a slow walk, then called out to a passerby, asking directions to the sheriff's office. Nodding his thanks, he headed for the office.

Hollister was at his desk and looked up when the federal circuit judge Kittering J. Barker stepped through the door slapping trail dust off his suit. The judge plopped his briefcase on the desk and introduced himself in his short, to-the-point manner sticking out a stubby hand. Then he pulled up a chair and sat down.

"I'm looking for a man named Raffe Latimer. Do you know him, or where I can find him?"

He pulled out a strong, black crook cigar and lit it, exhaling a cloud of blue smoke as he studied the sheriff's reaction to his question.

"Latimer . . . yeah, I know him. In fact, I'm looking for him myself, and I've got my deputy out right now looking to bring him in. There are even a few other people who've got their eye out for him. He's a dangerous man, and someone I'm going to put back behind bars one way or the other. What's your business with a murderer like that anyway?"

"My business is court business not to be discussed in detail except with this Latimer, at least initially. But I will go so far as to tell you this. He's filed for a review of his conviction and the sentence he served down in territorial prison, and he may have enough legal grounds to make it stick. When I find him I'm prepared to reconvene a hearing right here in Placer City and get to the bottom of his allegations, then decide if any further course of action would be required. Is there a rancher hereabouts named Cyrus Slaughter? That's someone else I'd like to sit down with."

For a moment, Hollister was so stunned at the suddenness of the judge's words that he only stared back with a blank expression on his face, his mind racing for answers.

"Slaughter . . . yes, he still lives here . . . just outside of town, but what's he got to do with any of this?"

"I won't go into that right now; I just want to know if the principals involved are available to me if I call them in, and of course I already know you're here and your deputy too. I'm going over to the hotel I passed down the street to get a room. If you find Mr. Latimer I want you to bring him to me immediately, do you understand?"

"Latimer's a murderer!" Hollister rose to his feet, eyes flashing in fear and hate. "You can't believe anything he says. He and his outlaw brothers killed three men in cold blood right out front on Main Street in front of witnesses. He'll lie through his teeth to save his skin. No one in his right mind would grant him a hearing. What he needs is a short trip to the gallows!"

Barker stood slowly, taking the cigar from his mouth, and leaned forward on the desk with both hands, eyes riveted on the sheriff.

"Mr. Hollister, I'm a federally appointed circuit court judge, and I expect you to carry out my orders without equivocation, do I make myself clear? I will decide what actions to take or not take and no one else. I didn't ride four days to get here, to then just turn around and go back to Loyalton without the answers to some very important questions. I want to settle these allegations once and for all. There may have been, and I emphasize the word 'may,' a gross injustice of law done to this man, and if I find that is the case, I mean to set it straight. Now, as I said, if and when you find him, you bring him to me, and in one piece. Do I make myself perfectly clear, Sheriff? Good day to you, sir!"

Hollister didn't answer, and simply dropped back down in the chair, nearly overwhelmed at even the hint of a reversal. If the setup they'd used to send Latimer to prison were ever revealed, along with the illegal land grab they'd made for Quiet Creek Ranch and its gold, they'd all end up behind bars, or maybe even worse. He decided then and there that he wasn't going to take the fall for Slaughter, Everheardt, or anyone else, and the only way to stop it before it got started was to kill Latimer before he could make any statements to Judge Barker. He had to find him now more than ever before. He got to his feet and went over to the gunrack, pulling down the sawed-off, .12-gauge double-barrel, then breaking the action open and dunking in two thumb-thick loads of buckshot.

Raffe pulled his horse to a stop above town meaning to meet Jennifer after work and surprise her. The afternoon sun was falling lower in the western sky as he looked down at the hazy smoke rising from several homes. The community was bathed in a pleasant golden glow and Raffe could hear the distant barking of a dog soft on the breeze as he urged his mount forward.

Johnny Quick was in his upstairs hotel room when he glanced out the window and saw the sheriff leave his office, shotgun under his arm, then stride down the street, grim-faced. He wondered what was going on, then slipped into his jacket, buckling his gun belt underneath it, and headed downstairs.

Raffe finally pulled his horse to a stop at the

livery stable near the edge of town. He had the owner, Tom Owens, take the big horse in, and then started toward Jennifer's apartment, staying off Main Street where he might be seen. A few minutes later Deputy Richie, hidden in alley shadows, saw him coming. Richie turned and ran for the office, only to see Hollister coming down the street toward him.

"Bart, Bart, he's here, Latimer's in town, back down there!" He pointed frantically as the sheriff started forward at a dead run.

"Where is he?" Hollister yelled, red-faced and breathing hard.

"Down in the alley—I think he's headed for Miss Mitchell's place. We've got him for sure this time, Bart!"

Both men turned and ran out of sight just as Jennifer exited the bank with Everheardt behind her. He locked the door and bid her goodbye, she started for home.

Raffe had just reached the apartment and turned to put the spare key in the lock, when a sharp voice rang out behind him.

"Don't even think of making a move, Latimer! Now, just get those hands up and turn around, real slow-like."

The sheriff stepped out from the shadows, a crooked smile across his sweaty face, the gaping double-barreled shotgun leveled at Raffe's middle.

"You've made your last trip into Placer City, you know that, don't you? Yeah, me and my deputy caught you here and you tried to escape and we had to cut you down to stop you, that's what it will be, and we did it for the good of the community, to uphold law and order. You know about law and order, don't you? That's what you get sent down to prison for, breaking the law, but this time the only place I'm going to send you is six feet straight down. Your days of causing me misery are over. Now, take your left hand and ease that six-gun out real slow and toss it over here."

Raffe's eyes never left Hollister as he lifted the big pistol clear of his holster and threw it. The lawman stepped forward, snuggling the ugly scatter-gun tight against his body, ready for the mule kick recoil, as his finger tightened on the trigger.

"Drop it!" Quick's slim silhouette framed the alley entrance twenty feet away. "Put it on the ground now, or I'll kill you where you stand. Right now, put it down!"

But Hollister suddenly spun and fired. Quick felt the hot thud of buckshot cut into him, and he went down with his six-gun blazing. Richie caught the bullets meant for the sheriff as Hollister ran by the stricken gunslinger out onto Main Street, directly into Jennifer Mitchell. Instantly he grabbed her, spinning her around to use as a shield and dragging her backwards down the street as Raffe emerged from the alley and came to a sudden stop.

"That's it, throw it down or I'll take off her head!" Hollister pressed the still hot barrels to Jennifer's neck. "I won't tell you again. Throw it down!"

Raffe stopped dead in his tracks, desperate to save her.

"Let her go if you've got an ounce of decency left in you. I'll take you on one-on-one, but leave her out of it. She's got nothing to do with what's between you and me. Let her go, Hollister!"

"Not a chance, now. She's my ticket out of here, and I just might take her with me to be sure nobody tries to follow me. Now get rid of the gun before I pull off one of these barrels and your precious girlfriend goes all to pieces over you. Do it!"

Raffe let the Colt slip from his fingers and stood motionless, now powerless to save her.

"That's right. Now I'm going to finish you off like I started to back there!" Hollister pulled Jennifer aside, swinging the shotgun toward Raffe as she struggled frantically, trying to stop him. "Goodbye, Latimer!"

A single shot rang out and Hollister suddenly stumbled back, dropping the scatter-gun and clutching at his throat. Jennifer broke free and ran for Raffe as the sheriff sank to his knees, blood flowing between his fingers, then pitched forward, face down. On the hotel porch behind him, Judge Barker lowered his little belt pistol. People streamed back out onto the street, yelling excitedly as they surrounded Raffe and Jennifer and then turning to look down at Hollister's prostate form. At long last vengeance had played out the final hand, and that hand had won.

A week later, the judge held a formal hearing on Raffe's petition and found in his favor, expunging all previous charges against him and returning Quiet Creek Ranch to its rightful owner. Both Cyrus Slaughter and Horace Everheardt were convicted of conspiracy to commit fraud and as accomplices to murder, and sentenced to fifteen years in the territorial prison. Neither man lived to serve out their time.

Johnny Quick lived, though his legs remained partially paralyzed and he was required to walk with a cane. He purchased one with a fancy carved ivory head and brass bottom peg.

When Raffe and Jennifer visited him just before he left town, he needled the big man just as he'd always enjoyed doing.

"You know, back there in that alley for a moment I really wasn't sure whether to let Hollister take you out or not. After all, I was considering collecting a three-thousand-dollar price tag on you. Darned if I didn't let my conscience get the best of me, and look what I got for it—useless legs."

He twirled the fancy walking stick round in his hands, a thin smile playing across his handsome face. "I guess I'm going to have to take up poker full-time now to make a living. I hope you're worth all this, preacher." Raffe reached over without comment to shake his hand in farewell.

The evening shadows draped the surrounding mountains in velvet blue as the first thin sliver of a lemon yellow moon floated up through the trees. Raffe wrapped his arms around Jennifer as they stood on the porch of Quiet Creek Ranch.

"You do know that we've got a whole lot of work to do to bring this place back, don't you?"

"Yes." She turned to face him, kissing him long and hard on the mouth before pulling back and holding his face with both hands. "But we've got a lifetime to do it in now . . . and we will."

The End